Copyright © 2016 by Mattel, Inc.
All rights reserved. EVER AFTER HIGH and associated trademarks
are owned by and used under license from Mattel, Inc.

In accordance with the U.S. Copyright Act of 1976, the scanning, uploading, and
electronic sharing of any part of this book without the permission
of the publisher is unlawful piracy and theft of the author's intellectual
property. If you would like to use material from the book (other than for review
purposes), prior written permission must be obtained by contacting the
publisher at permissions@hbgusa.com. Thank you for your support of the
author's rights.

Little, Brown and Company

Hachette Book Group
1290 Avenue of the Americas, New York, NY 10104
Visit us at lb-kids.com

Little, Brown and Company is a division of Hachette Book Group, Inc.
The Little, Brown name and logo are trademarks of Hachette Book Group, Inc.

The publisher is not responsible for websites (or their content) that
are not owned by the publisher.

First Edition: February 2016

Library of Congress Control Number: 2015955793

Junior Novel Paperback ISBN 978-0-316-30184-8
Deluxe Junior Novel ISBN 978-0-316-27045-8

10 9 8 7 6 5 4 3 2 1

RRD-C

Printed in the United States of America

Ever After High™

DRAGON GAMES

The Junior Novel

by Stacia Deutsch

Based on the screenplay written by
Sherry Klein, Shadi Petrosky, and Keith Wagner

LITTLE, BROWN AND COMPANY
New York Boston

CHAPTER 1

It was the most important day ever after. Raven Queen's purple-and-black skirt swished and her shoes clicked a rapid staccato against the Ever After High School floors as she dashed down the long hallway. Cedar, Daring, Blondie, Sparrow, Cerise, Briar, and Hopper all rushed to catch up. It wasn't easy. Raven was moving fast.

"This was no ordinary day for Raven Queen, the daughter of the Evil Queen. This was *the* day!" a Male Narrator explained.

A Female Narrator added, "Raven was finally mastering her magic. Only she wasn't using her powers in a way that would please her evil mother."

Brooke Page was part of the conversation as well. She

remarked, "Well, you know what they say—you can't judge a book by its mother."

The Female Narrator, who happened to be Brooke's mother, laughed at the clever wordplay. "Cute, Brooke."

———

Cedar Wood, Pinocchio's daughter, reached Raven first. "Raven, glad I caught you!" Cedar raised her hand. "I broke a nail and gave myself a splinter!"

With a quick wave, Raven shot sparks of purple light from her fingers and—*poof!*—nail fixed, splinter gone. "No problem, Cedar. Good as new!" Raven said.

Cedar studied her manicure and smiled. "Wow! Thanks, Raven!"

Raven kept walking briskly. The sound of her heels echoed down the hallway.

Goldilocks's daughter, Blondie Lockes, caught up next. She held up a MirrorPad with a cracked screen. Breathless from chasing Raven, she said, "I dropped my MirrorPad, and now I can't record my MirrorCast this afternoon!"

Zap! With a blast from her fingers, Raven fixed the MirrorPad. She didn't even have to stop walking. Blondie held the MirrorPad to her chest and grinned gratefully.

Daring Charming, one of King and Queen Charming's sons, also had a request for Raven. He scooted up next to her with his hand over his mouth. Raven gave him a quick glance and could see he was embarrassed about something.

"I toasted marshmallows with dragon fire, and the soot

stained my teeth!" Daring moved his hand away to show her his black-stained smile.

With a small nod, Raven flicked her wrist and once again—*poof!* His teeth were as blindingly white as ever.

Daring brought out his jeweled hand mirror and beamed at his reflection. Raven blinked hard from the glare.

With each step she took, the group that followed Raven down the hallway grew. It seemed as if every student at Ever After High needed her right at that very moment.

"Raven, help me!"

"I'm next!"

"My turn!"

Raven told them, "Okay, you guys, as much as I would love to, I can't do spells all day—" Near the end of the long hallway, there was a flash of red. Apple White, the daughter of Snow White, was walking slowly in her direction. Apple's shiny, well-conditioned blond curls bounced with each step.

Raven grabbed her. "Apple! I'm so late! *You-know-who* is going to have an epic meltdown!" Raven's eyes were wide with panic.

"Go, go, go!" Apple said. "I've got this."

Raven was grateful. "Really? I owe you one, Apple."

Apple smiled a vivid white smile, not as dazzling as Daring's, but close. "That's what friends forever after are for," she said.

Raven didn't wait another second. She escaped down the hall and fled around the corner.

Blocking the hallway, Apple intercepted Tiny and the Three Billy Goats. All three goats had managed to get their heads stuck in one of the Giant's oversize jelly jars.

"The Billy Goats are in a jam...and it's my jam!" Tiny exclaimed, stomping his gigantic foot.

"I'd be happy to help," Apple said, surveying the situation.

The Billy Goats bleated, "We need Raven—not *you*!" Their voices were muffled inside the jar.

Apple sighed. This was not going to be easy....

Raven entered another hall and hurried past Darling Charming. Darling was playing cards with Lizzie Hearts, the daughter of the Queen of Hearts, taking turns throwing them one by one into the hat of Madeline Hatter. Madeline just so happened to be the daughter of the Mad Hatter, and the fancy hat she was holding was one of many from her large collection of hats.

"Good luck today!" Lizzie called after Raven.

"Have a wonderlandiful visit!" Maddie added.

"And keep away from the glass!" Darling warned.

Raven gave them a quick wave. "Thanks, guys."

Ever After's Male Narrator tracked her movements. "Visiting Day. The day Raven gets to see her mother in her mirror prison." He paused before adding dramatically, "And Raven was nervous."

Brooke replied, "I'd be nervous, too, if my mom were the Evil Queen."

———

Raven turned down a foreboding corridor and slowed her steps until she stopped in front of a thick, heavy wooden door. She took a breath to steady herself before entering.

Milton Grimm, the headmaster of Ever After High, was sitting at a table, holding a clipboard. "Ms. Queen," he greeted, handing her a quill. "Sign here and here and here. Now, remember, keep away—"

"From the glass. I know, I know." Raven raised the quill and signed her name in triplicate.

The door she had to enter next was boarded up and tied down with crisscrossing chains. A large purple dragon was blocking the way. When Raven approached, the dragon rose from the shadows, growing to her full height and roaring loudly.

Raven wasn't afraid of Nevermore. Nevermore was her pet dragon, after all, here to protect her. It was what was behind that door that was scary. Raven stepped up to the ferocious beast and tickled her belly. Nevermore shrank to the size of a puppy, rolled over, and purred like a kitten.

Raven gave her a little tummy rub. "Nevermore! Who's a good dragon?" She looked toward the chained doorway and said confidently, "Don't worry. I can handle Mom."

Nevermore grew a little larger, now as big as a medium-sized dog, and moved next to Raven so they were facing the door together. Raven raised her hands. Purple laser beams shot out from her fingertips, and—*zap!*—the chains popped off. Raven pushed open the protective door and, with Nevermore by her side, climbed the spiral staircase to the mysterious tower attic.

CHAPTER 2

The attic had cobwebs along the ceiling, in the corners, and atop the piles of junk around the dusty room. Slats of light filtered through rotten boards, creating spooky shadows on old blackboards, broken desks, and faded-yellow school supplies, long left behind. In the center of the room was the thing Raven was looking for: the magic mirror.

Raven had managed to keep her nerves in check until this moment. She shivered as she stepped up to the mirror and saw the reflective glass shimmer like water in a pond.

"Hi, Mom," Raven said, swallowing hard. "It's me."

In a puff of purple vapor, the Evil Queen materialized in the mirror's reflection. She was wearing a sweat suit while working out on an exercise bicycle. The queen smiled a wicked grin when she saw her daughter.

"Raven! There's my little blackbird!" she said cheerfully. "I've been waiting forever after! Did you miss me? How do

I look?" The Evil Queen raised one arched eyebrow unnaturally high.

Trying not to stare at the odd eyebrow, Raven pressed her lips together. These conversations were always a little awkward. "You look great, Mom."

"How's school?" the Evil Queen asked. "Have you been a bad girl?"

Raven searched her brain for something her mom would like to hear. "I should tell you I cast a horrible spell on my roommate, Apple White."

"Now, that's what I like to hear!" The queen was impressed.

But then Raven said, "I should...but I didn't." She shrugged. This evil stuff just wasn't in Raven's nature.

"Oh, what's the use in pretending?" her mother said with a sigh. "I know you've been using your powers for good, helping others." She shook her head. "Where did I go wrong?"

"I'm happy," Raven said. "People like me, Mom."

The queen frowned. "No one ever took over the world by being nice." She paused her workout and stared through the mirror at Raven. "Harness your evil before it's too late, young lady."

That wasn't Raven's style. "Things have changed, Mom. It's not like back when you went to school here. We can choose our own destiny."

The queen snorted. "I know one thing hasn't changed: It's better to be feared than forgotten." She pointed a finger at Raven and asked, "How long have I been stuck in this mirror, and I'm still witch and famous?"

"It's true," Raven reluctantly agreed. "Everybody fears you."

"Thank you!" Her mother leaned in to the magic mirror's frame. "Get me out of here, and I'll show you the way. We'll rule side by side. It'll be a great bonding experience." She laughed. "Like shopping, only world domination. We'll take over Ever After High together."

Raven took a step back. "Take over the school? Why would I want to hurt my friends? Don't you get it? I *never* want to be like you!" She paused and then proclaimed, "I want to choose my own Happily Ever After!"

The Evil Queen could actually see the anger coursing through her blood.

Raven balled her fists and reared back, when suddenly Nevermore popped up. She was a little bigger than she'd been when Raven left her outside.

Oh...

She closed her eyes as she realized that her mother had very nearly tricked her. Nevermore had stopped her from making a terrible mistake.

The Evil Queen hissed.

Nevermore shrank down to puppy size and quickly ran to hide behind a pile of paint cans. She moved so fast the cans tipped, dumping paint everywhere. Raven scooped up the wet and color-coated dragon and cradled her like a baby.

Turning to the mirror, Raven said, "Nice try, Mom. You

want me to break the mirror. You're not getting out that easily."

The crash of the paint cans had alerted Headmaster Grimm, who stormed into the room.

The queen shrugged. "Can't blame an evil queen for trying."

Grimm cleared his throat. "Visiting hours are over!"

Raven turned on her heel and walked away without looking back. Nevermore, however, peeked over Raven's shoulder and growled at the queen.

She growled back, then threatened, "Oh, I'll find a way to break this mirror. And then Ever After High will be facing a lot worse than seven years of bad luck.... Count on it."

CHAPTER 3

Raven found her friends by the school lockers. She cradled the pint-sized Nevermore in her arms. The dragon was covered in bright paint, looking very sad.

"I know exactly how you feel," Raven said as she set her on the ground. Nevermore snuggled against Raven's ankle.

Holly and Poppy O'Hair, the twin daughters of Rapunzel, bounced up to Raven with their usual enthusiasm.

"Hey, Raven," Poppy greeted. "How was Visiting Day?" She knelt down to scratch Nevermore's neck.

Holly examined the mini-dragon and asked, "What happened to you, girl?"

Raven shook her head. "Don't ask."

Nevermore lowered her head, and big splotches of paint dripped onto the floor.

"Someone sure needs a bath!" Poppy said, staring down at the rainbow-colored puddle.

Just as Raven was starting to tell the twins what had happened in the attic, Blondie and Apple joined the group. "My mom really spooked Nevermore," Raven told them. "And, well—you can see she wound up with a bit of a messy makeover."

With a miserable little sigh, Nevermore dribbled more paint around her feet.

Raven said, "I tried to magic the paint off, but I just turned it to this—" She waved her hand and Nevermore's colors glowed brighter.

"Grooming? Sounds like a job for Holly and Poppy!" Poppy said.

"The O'Hair twins!" Holly exclaimed. "We can groom Nevermore for you!"

Raven was appreciative, but Nevermore looked less sure. She grew slightly, from the size of a puppy to that of a small dog, as they led her away for a bath.

CHAPTER 4

The Female Narrator said, "There she is—Queen of the Land, the Fairest of Them All, the mother of Apple White...."

The Male Narrator added, "*The* Snow White. She's also a very powerful royal executive. She employs over seven hundred dwarves!"

"Wow, she's a total spellebrity!" Brooke Page announced as a pumpkin stretch limo pulled up in front of a beautiful castle and the chauffeur opened the queen's door. A dwarf helped Snow White out onto the pavement.

The Fairest of All Queens sauntered at a royal pace down a red carpet, then up a long white marble staircase into her sparkling castle. As she went, her dwarf business assistants handed her parchments with proclamations written in fancy script for her signature. Several bluebirds hovered around Snow White, chirping compliments in her ears.

Snow White laughed. In a high-pitched voice, she told the birds, "What a sweet thing to say. Your queen loves you, too!" Then, with precise movements, she turned to one of the dwarves at her side. "How's the enchanted-cape collection selling?"

The dwarf held up a foam board covered with sales numbers and a large arrow pointing up.

"Hexcellent," Snow said. "My daughter will live comfortably ever after." She asked another dwarf, "By the way, how is Apple doing in school?"

The dwarf showed her a different chart. It revealed that Apple had high marks.

"Straight A's! Perfect." She asked another dwarf, "What about socially? How are her ratings?"

This dwarf pushed up his glasses and raised a Popularity Flowchart. Raven's arrow was up. Way up. But Apple's was down. Way down.

"Apple's popularity is down?" Snow's voice dropped octaves to a deep growl that caused the birds to tremble and fly away. "My daughter?" She pointed at the board. "And who is—Raven? This is fairy, fairy bad news!"

A dwarf anticipated that Snow would want her Mirror-Phone. He handed it to her right away.

Apple White was at her desk doing thronework when her MirrorPhone rang. She peeked at the caller ID: MOM.

"Once upon a hi, Mom!" Apple answered in a cheery voice.

Snow White popped up on the chat screen. "Apple, I am fairy concerned about you." She glanced around the dorm room as best she could from inside the phone. "Is that a sock on the floor? An untidy room leads to an untidy fairytale!"

Apple quickly stuffed the sock into a laundry hamper. "Um, you called to tell me to clean my room?"

"No." She paused, then said, "There's no easy way to say this, Apple pie, but...your popularity is down thirteen percent!"

"I can explain!" Apple panicked. "It's Raven's fault." She gave her mom a pouty face, lower lip trembling. "Everyone likes her now that she's using her powers for good. Mom, it's terrible!"

Snow leaned in and filled the screen. "You need to be proactive, my little dove. Remind the world of our fairytale. Perhaps there's some way you could nudge Raven toward evil?"

"Raven's not like that," Apple insisted. Raven had decided to forge her own destiny and not become evil like her mom. "And I wouldn't do that." Apple was resigned to live with the consequences of Raven's decision.

Snow chuckled, a low rumble from her throat. "Remember, she's still her mother's daughter. And so are you. I named you Apple because that poisoned piece of fruit was the best thing that ever happened to me! It's how I met your father. And now I'm queen of the entire kingdom. So ask yourself: How badly do you want your Happily Ever After?" She left the question hanging for Apple to consider.

"Mom, you know how much I heart our family tradition!" Apple said honestly. She gave her mom a "What can I do?" look.

"Sometimes destiny needs a push, my sweet," Snow said. "Tell a little White lie if you must. I'll see what I can do from here to give you a boost."

Apple really did want to live Happily Ever After, but she didn't want to lie to get it. She said, "I'll think about it, Mom."

They hung up.

Apple was staring at her phone, thinking about her mother's call, when the door burst open and Raven came into the room they shared. Apple tossed the phone into a drawer as if Raven somehow knew what had just happened. She tried not to look suspicious.

"Hi, Raven—how was seeing your mom? Are you feeling any eviler?" Apple asked.

Raven plopped down on her bed. "What? No! Maybe. I don't know. My mom does make me want to scream sometimes."

"That's good! Maybe scream, and then explode something with dark magic." Apple made a few suggestions of things Raven could blow up.

"Hmm." Raven considered how Apple was acting. Her friend hadn't nagged her about being evil for a while. "Sounds like I'm not the only princess who got an earful from her mom today. So how is Mrs. White?"

Apple sighed and leaned back in her chair. "Once a ruler, always a ruler. She's worried I'm not following in her fairy-tale footsteps."

"That's the one thing your mom and my mom can agree on," Raven said with a matching sigh.

Raven glanced at Nevermore's cozy little dragon bed on the floor. It was empty because the twins were keeping her overnight for grooming. She looked at the empty cushions and wished her precious pet was there.

Apple couldn't sleep. After staring at the ceiling for a while, she gave up and went over to the big mirror on their dorm room wall. She stared at her reflection. "Mirror, mirror on the wall—why is life so unfairest after all?"

From behind the mirror, the Evil Queen heard every-thing. With a wave of her hands, she created a floating apple.

Suddenly, a waft of purple smoke magically materialized, and the magical apple passed through the mirror. A voice whispered, "Follow me...."

Apple was shocked! The mirror answered! The mirror was going to help her! She didn't hesitate. Apple followed the apple to an enchanted tree. With a quick look around to make sure no one saw, she stepped inside a doorway that had appeared in the tree.

The instant she entered the room, Apple knew she was in the tower attic. The large magic mirror in the center gave it away. She shouldn't be there.

"Why, Apple White. You poor thing," the Evil Queen said in her kindest voice. "Come, tell me your troubles."

Apple gasped and stumbled back. "You're...I can't talk to you."

"Oh, Apple, we have so much more in common than you know," the queen said.

Apple refused to believe that was true. "What do you want?"

"The same thing you want! For Raven to straighten up and fly right—or fly wrong, in our case. I could help you, you know," the queen said. "I can restore things to the good old ways, steer Raven on her course of evil so you get your Happily Ever After. But I can't do it from inside the mirror."

Apple squinted at the queen and said, "Even if I trusted you, I can't let you out of the mirror—that would be wrong."

"I see. I've made a mistake." The queen's voice dripped with disappointment. "I thought maybe you were like your mother. Snow White is a classic princess. When her time came, your mother embraced her fairytale destiny. She did whatever it took."

That made Apple angry. She wanted to be like her mom.

She wanted the destiny planned for her! Raven had messed everything up. In a surge of resentment over what she'd lost, Apple declared, "I will do whatever it takes!"

"Your mother was never afraid to go after her dreams." The queen's voice stayed low, constant, like an arrow that went straight to Apple's heart. "I guess the apple can fall pretty far from the tree."

"I'm not afraid, and I am like my mother!" Apple's voice echoed around the room. "My destiny is *mine!*" She hurled the ruby-red apple at the mirror with all her might.

The mirror shattered into bright shards of light. Flowing purple smoke filled the room as the Evil Queen exploded out of the glass! She was wearing her royal robes and her crown. Stretching out her arms, raising her staff, the queen cackled a harsh and violent laugh. She was free at last!

Apple's ears filled with the chaotic chuckle. Her vision was blurred by the shimmering purple smoke and the blinding light that reflected off the shards of shattered glass.

Apple was truly scared.

What had she done?

CHAPTER 5

The smoke dissipated, and Apple stood in the fading light, face-to-face with the Evil Queen.

The queen took a long breath, then let it out. "*Ah!* The air of that mirror prison was ever after so stuffy." From the mirror shards, she picked up the apple that had freed her.

Apple White was truly petrified.

The queen checked her reflection in a large mirror shard. She fixed her hair and grinned. "Years in a mirror prison without a single reflective surface to gaze at myself upon—now, that's torture."

Apple looked frantically toward the stairs. "I'm sorry. I need to go. I...I can't help you."

The queen laughed. "Too late. You broke me out of there! You want your friends or your mother to know you released *the Evil Queen*?" Feeling stiff from all those years trapped in mirror prison, she casually began to do some stretches.

"You can't just walk into school and talk to Raven!" Apple said, facing the reality of what she'd done. "What's going to happen when somebody recognizes you?"

That made the queen pause. "Good point. I'll need to reinvent my look to blend in with today's teens. Let's make some magic." She cleared her throat and dramatically raised her staff.

> *"From old to young,*
> *A journey back.*
> *To fit in would be prudent.*
> *Erase what time's cruel hands*
> *have done.*
> *Make me a high school*
> *student!"*

Lightning flashed as an electric vortex of purple smoke billowed around her. And *presto!*

Apple couldn't believe her eyes. The Evil Queen was now a teen queen.

"Ta-da! I suppose I'll need a new name to go with my new look." She checked out her new, stylish outfit and young, hip hairdo in the mirror shard. "How about Mira. Mira Shards." The Evil Queen laughed hysterically at her choice.

"Wow. Impressive! I'm speechless," Apple said. And she really was.

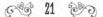

21

"I'm good. And by *good*, I mean *bad*." Mira crossed the room and linked her arm through Apple's. "Ready, my new BFFA? Time to go back to high school. Let's do this!"

Holly and Poppy were washing Nevermore in a special station they'd set up in the school's dragon stalls.

Poppy was sitting on the stall's wood-planked floor, shampooing little Nevermore in a basin of foamy water. Nevermore's long tail stuck out over the side.

Holly peeked over her sister's shoulder. "Wow, Poppy, this paint is hard to get off. You have to really scrub hard...." Holly moved in to help and accidentally stepped on the dragon's tail.

Nevermore roared and began to grow.

"Aaah! What's happening?" Poppy leaped back.

Nevermore grew and grew until the basin fit her like a shoe, and then she grew a little more until the basin got stuck on one clawed foot. In a panic, the dragon flew around the barn with the basin shoe, shaking dirty, soapy water all over Holly.

"My hair!" Holly screamed. "Bad dragon! Heel! Sit!"

Nevermore had a dragon tantrum and tossed anything she could find in the stall at Holly and Poppy.

"Dragons are dangerous business!" Holly said, ducking and dodging.

Poppy passed Holly a trash can lid to use as a shield. "Here, Holly, catch! Use this!"

Holly held the shield protectively in front of her as Nevermore's tail continued to swish violently, causing havoc. "Poppy," she told her sister, "we're going to need some kind of armor if we're going to stay in the dragon-grooming biz."

At lunch, Apple sat with Mira at a Castleteria table.

When the others came to sit, Apple said, "Everyone, I want you to meet the new girl—my, uh, old friend, uh, Mira!"

"What's down?" Mira greeted everyone cheerfully.

Apple leaned over and whispered in her ear.

"Up," Mira corrected quickly. "What's up? New friends."

Darling Charming and Cerise Hood, the daughter of Little Red Riding Hood, immediately started asking questions.

"I'm Darling, Darling Charming. How do you guys know each other?" She pointed from Apple to Mira.

"Neighbors," Apple said.

"Camp," Mira said at the exact same time. "We went to neighboring camps," Mira corrected.

"I'm Cerise Hood. What school did you—"

Mira interrupted. "I was homeschooled."

Darling said, "Sounds so isolated."

Mira gave a small laugh. "Darling, you have no idea."

A small group of girls came up then. They all wanted to know about Mira's trendy fashion style.

"Hi, I'm Ashlynn," Ashlynn Ella, the daughter of

Cinderella, said with a warm smile. She introduced the others. "That's Lizzie and Briar. We love your outfit!" Lizzie Hearts and Briar Beauty, daughter of Sleeping Beauty, nodded enthusiastically.

Raven joined them, telling Mira, "You look wicked." For a second, Mira gave a strange, worried expression, but then Raven said, "Wicked awesome!"

Mira visibly relaxed. "You must be Raven Queen! You're, like, a spellebrity! Daughter of the greatest villain in all of fairytale history!" she gushed. "I mean, wow."

Raven shrugged. "My mother's a controlling drama queen."

There was a twinkle in Mira's eye as she said, "Thank you!"

Apple had to cover for Mira's joy at being called evil. She quickly blurted out, "That's exactly what Mira says."

Mira and Raven shared a smile, knowing they had controlling mothers in common. The connection made Raven like Mira.

Before they could get to know one another better, Holly and Poppy arrived carrying Nevermore, who had shrunk back to puppy size. She smelled sweet and was all dressed up in bows.

"Well, what do you think?" Poppy asked Raven.

"Nevermore!" She took a long look, then slowly said, "She looks very…"

Holly chuckled. "Bow-dacious! Ha! Get it?"

That was when Nevermore saw Mira and recognized the

Evil Queen in disguise. In a flash, Nevermore ballooned to her full, giant, mighty dragon size! Her long, thick dragon tail scattered the tables and chairs as she desperately tried to escape from the Castleteria. Students scrambled to get out of her way.

Nevermore stumbled into the salad bar, spraying food everywhere. Her clean bows dripped with lettuce, veggies, and dressing.

Headmaster Grimm marched into the room. "Raven Queen, what is your animal doing in the Castleteria? This is a disgrace, not to mention a health-code violation!"

Raven stood, and Nevermore immediately shrank down to her smallest size. Raven scooped her up. "I'm sorry, Headmaster Grimm. It won't happen again!" Head lowered, Raven held her pet close as she left the room.

CHAPTER 6

Mira caught up with Raven in the hallway. Raven was holding Nevermore as if she were burping a baby, high over her shoulder. The dragon continued to growl at Mira, staring at her with knowing eyes.

Mira acted as if the dragon was the most adorable thing she'd ever seen.

Raven apologized. "I don't know what has gotten into Nevermore. She doesn't normally spook like that! Hush, girl!"

"Let me help," Mira said. "I have a way with dragons." Behind Raven's back, Mira's eyes flashed red as the queen zapped the dragon with a small purple shock. Nevermore whimpered and burrowed her face into Raven's shoulder, suddenly calm.

"She quieted right down! That was great. Thanks!" Raven said.

Mira shrugged, as if all she'd done was pet the dragon.

"That was unfairest of Grimm to bust you like that. Why didn't you blame Holly and Poppy? They brought the dragon into the Castleteria!"

Raven raised a shoulder and said, "That's not what friends do." They'd reached the end of the hall. "Well, I'd better get to Science and Sorcery class. Thanks again for your help with Nevermore, Mira."

Mira pretended to look at her schedule. "Actually—I'm in that class. In fact, I bet we have lots of the same classes." She followed Raven around the corner. "Maybe you could show me the ropes?"

"Sure! I love to help," Raven said, leading the way.

A few paces back, Apple watched Mira and Raven. When Raven agreed to show her mother around, Apple smiled to herself. This plan was going to work. Her own fairytale destiny would be back on track in no time.

The hours went by quickly. Raven gave Mira a tour of the school. They went to Raven's room and hung out for a while.

By the time General Villainy began, Raven and Mira were becoming fast friends. Raven blew a kiss to Nevermore, then shut the door. The girls ran off to class, giggling all the way.

At the beginning of the period, Mr. Badwolf handed back the students' tests.

"Here are your General Villainy hexam results." He set a graded sheet on Raven's desk and said, "Room for improvement, Miss Queen." The page was covered with bright red X's.

Mira leaned over and whispered, "Cast a spell on the teacher and get straight A's. That's what I did in school."

Raven looked at her, confused. "I thought you were homeschool—"

Mr. Badwolf interrupted with a mighty roar. "*Ladies!* Talking in class?" He'd heard Mira's suggestion. "Encouraging cheating?" He squinted at her. "Wicked girls!" Mr. Badwolf directed his attention to Raven, saying, "Raven, stick with this new girl—you could learn a thing or two." He winked at them both.

Raven and Mira paused for a beat, then laughed.

At dinner that night in the Castleteria, Darling and Cerise approached Mira, Raven, and Apple, and were about to sit down when Mira put out her hands to stop them. "We were saving these seats. Sorry."

Stunned and confused, Darling and Cerise walked away.

Raven turned to Mira. "That wasn't fairy nice. Darling and Cerise are my friends!"

Mira snorted. "Nice will only get you so far. To be really popular, you need a little fear factor. Right, Apple?"

Apple considered it and said, "I suppose there's truth in that."

Raven, suspicious, raised an eyebrow.

Holly and Poppy then came to the table. They were wearing protective dragon armor that they'd clearly made themselves. It was as if they'd raided the school-supply closet and used anything they could find, from textbooks to trash cans. Their hodgepodge armor was covered in soot.

"Raven, don't freak out," Poppy began, "but we were trying this new scale polish on Nevermore, and, well, she took off."

Holly explained, "We set up a grooming station in the old dragon stables behind the school. That's the last place we saw her. We thought, maybe if you call her—"

"—maybe she's just hiding and would come out! We're sorry." Poppy looked like she was about to cry.

"Thanks for getting me," Raven said. She gathered her stuff. "Let's go."

They had come so far, and yet the plan wasn't working. Raven continued to be a huge disappointment to villains everywhere!

Raven went with Mira, Apple, Poppy, and Holly to the dragon stables behind the school. Beyond the crumbling stables was a weed-covered circular area.

Raven took a long look at the field. "Wow! Can you believe I've never been back here before? The old Dragon Games arena."

Mira clapped in excitement. "Dragon Games sound wicked! Have you ever played? You do have a dragon!"

"No, I know," she said. "But my mom was a champion at it. I kind of don't want to do anything like her."

Mira frowned as a shadow of sadness passed across her face. Raven's words had cut her like a sharp sword.

The girls didn't notice.

"Why did Headmaster Grimm close the Dragon Center?" Apple asked her friends.

"You mean you don't know?" Holly was shocked. She powered up her MirrorPad and handed it to Poppy, who brought up the video.

The recording was grainy and slow to load. It showed two rival riders on dragonback from a few decades ago. They were both wearing helmets and zooming at each other in a heated aerial battle.

"They used to ride dragons right here." Holly pointed out to the weed patch. "Dragon Games were all the rage."

"They say Snow White and the Evil Queen were the greatest Dragon Games captains ever after..." Poppy added. "But they were terribly competitive. Dragon Games can be fairy dangerous. I read that the old school mascot, Legend, used to compete and is the only dragon left from that brood—"

Whatever else she was going to say was cut off when the girls heard a terrible moan.

"That's a dragon cry," Mira told the others. "I'd know it anywhere."

"Nevermore? Hurry!" Raven ran toward the stalls, in the direction of the moan, leading the others to follow.

Daring Charming was already in a stall. He was on his knees, leaning over a huge dragon. It wasn't Nevermore, but rather the school's mascot, Legend. The dragon was thrashing, rolling around, and moaning.

As the girls all rushed in, Daring told them, "Something's wrong with Legend! I went to saddle him up for our morning ride, and he won't fly."

The twins sprang into paramedic mode.

"Quick, check the tongue color!" Poppy told Holly.

Holly pried the dragon's mouth open to find a darting green tongue. Legend rolled over in discomfort. Holly jumped back just in time, saying, "Body temperature seems really high!"

Apple was amazed. "Fairy impressive! You two have really learned a lot about dragons lately."

Legend shifted again, and the dragon's painful moans got even louder. The twins set a claw-mometer over a front paw.

"Subzero," Holly reported.

"Oh no! My trusty steed! Does that mean he's really sick?" Daring asked, face panicked.

"News flash, Daring. Your trusty steed isn't a he. She's a *she*! And she's not sick...." Mira smiled.

The girls all understood what she was saying, but Daring's face looked blank. *"Huh?"*

"I think it's time...." Holly pushed Daring out of the way and moved in closer.

"What time?" Daring asked. Suddenly, he clued in. "Oh, *that* time!" Daring swooned, and Mira had to catch him before he hit the floor.

Legend began to lay eggs. Lots and lots of eggs. Some were white, some dark, all were going to hatch into baby dragons.

Blondie stuck her head in the barn and saw the eggs. She rushed off to grab her microphone and start spreading the news.

"Yes!" Poppy was super excited. More than her usual amount. "Dragon egg season! Oh my fairy godmother, this is hexciting!"

Holly read from her MirrorPad. "Dragonpedia says that in the wild, mothers lay their eggs near active volcanoes to warm them until they hatch! It takes years, apparently."

Raven said, "I could cast a spell to keep the eggs warm. *Incubation incantation, warm with lava imitation!*" Light shot from Raven's fingers and—*zap!*—it was warm enough to care for the twelve eggs in the soft hay.

When Raven was distracted, Mira whispered, "This spell could use a power-up."

With a *zap!* of her own, Mira sent a current along the ground and toward the eggs. They suddenly glowed much brighter—so bright and hot, in fact, that the girls had to shield their eyes.

Raven tried to figure out what had gone wrong. "Oh no! I must have overdone it!"

Crack!—an egg began to hatch. Then another. And another.

Precious baby dragons began crawling out of their eggs, into the light, and blinking open their moist little eyes. They stretched their tiny wings and steadied themselves on their feet.

"This is bad. It got *too* hot!" Holly said, looking at the dragons. "That can make them turn..."

"Evil!" Apple finished, turning to face Mira.

Mira simply smiled and said to Raven, "What are you trying to do, Raven, you wicked girl? Trying to make evil dragons?"

"Me? Never! Who would do such a thing?" Raven shook her head.

"Your mother," Mira muttered, but no one heard.

The girls all looked at Raven with doubt. Raven raised her hands. This was not her fault. Just then, Nevermore, in her medium-sized-dog body, peeked around the corner.

Raven was relieved to see her. "Nevermore! There you are! Look at all these new friends for you!"

Nevermore stepped forward to investigate, but she leaped back when one of the little dark ones hissed at her.

Brooke Page said, "The Evil Queen would totally do such a thing. And she just did."

"True, but perhaps Raven's taking the blame will help get this fairytale back on course," the Female Narrator suggested.

"I say, dragons at Ever After High!" the Male Narrator said. "One thing is certain: This is the greatest threat our young heroines have ever faced."

CHAPTER 7

This is Blondie Lockes, reporting live at Ever After High, where dragons once again roam the hallowed halls, ending the long-standing ban on the controversial Dragon Games program."

Blondie reported the news while Holly and Poppy fed the baby dragons. New dragons meant new armor. They brought the dragons fresh vegetables in a large basket. The instant they saw the food, the babies scarfed it down as fast as Holly and Poppy could hand it out.

"Ow!" Holly exclaimed when one hungry baby accidentally nipped her finger.

Blondie went on with the news report. She looked at her shoulder, where a baby dragon was nibbling on her hair. "It would seem the students of Ever After High are eager to adopt these pesky pets...."

Darling's dragon breathed ice. She held out a paper cone, and he shot a breath of snow onto it. Instant snow cone!

Holly and Poppy took two babies back to the dorm, where they jumped on the bed. One breathed fire. The other ice. Fire. Ice. Fire. Ice. Together, they made steam!

Madeline Hatter's dragon had an amazing talent. She breathed a web of pink cotton candy that wrapped around Maddie's hat. "Cotton candy! Yum!" Maddie was thrilled as she bit into the sugar and licked her lips.

Apple's room was cold—that was, until her dragon shot fire into the fireplace, lighting the logs. She rubbed her hands together near the flame and said, "Good girl."

Behind the stables, while everyone was getting to know their new pets, Mira used her "charms" to persuade Nevermore to let her ride her. Together, they flew up, perched for a long moment on a brick wall, then swooped toward the ground. In a swift move, Mira made the dragon's tail spiral, creating a corkscrew. Mira completed two full aerial rotations before landing gracefully. As she dismounted, she triumphantly punched the air.

"Raven, you have to try this. Nevermore is a natural! Woo!"

Blondie closed her MirrorCast by asking her viewers: "What will become of Dragon Games? Only time will tell."

Snow White was working on papers and signing scrolls when she saw Blondie's news flash. Her eyes lit up as she recognized her nemesis performing tricks on the dragon!

"Why, you wicked old thing!" She laughed. "Welcome back. Hmmm." A brilliant thought came to her. "*Summon the architects!*" she shouted to a dwarf down the hall. "I've just had the fairest idea of all." She smiled to herself, saying, "This should get Apple back on top—and freshen my pure-as-snow image, too!"

"What is with the sudden assembly?" Mira asked Raven as they searched for seats in the Ever After High Charmitorium.

"It's top secret. No one knows," Raven answered.

"I heard there's a special guest!" Blondie said.

"This is hexciting!" Apple said as they all found seats together.

Headmaster Grimm took the stage. "It is my honor to welcome back our favorite and most successful graduate, the ruler of our kingdom—our beloved queen, Snow White!" He stepped aside as Apple's mom entered the room.

The students and teachers all started to applaud, except for Apple. She looked at her mom's bodyguard dwarves and the fluttering bluebirds, and wondered what was going on. "Uh-oh...Mom?"

Snow White waited until the clapping stopped, then

stood behind the podium. "A little bird told me that dragons have returned to my beloved alma mater. So it's time we restored the good old ways. Today, Dragon Games are reinstated at Ever After High."

The students cheered, while Grimm and other teachers looked nervous.

Snow White went on. "Dragon Games are tough yet elegant. And I want my Ever After High riders dressed accordingly. Girls?"

There was a gasp that rose from the crowd as MirrorPhone flashes recorded pictures of this historic moment.

"I've hired the creative team of Lizzie Hearts and Ashlynn Ella to design all-new Dragon Games wear," Snow White said.

Lizzie and Ashlynn stepped forward to present their models: Holly and Poppy crossed the stage, sporting fabulous riding-armor uniforms—

After the applause died down, Lizzie and Ashlynn held up drawings for additional designs, specially created for Apple and Raven.

"These looks are lightweight, flexible, and fashion-forward," Lizzie said.

Ashlynn told the students more about the uniforms, saying, "Not to mention fireproof, ice-proof, and explosion-resistant!"

The students were all impressed and applauded loudly.

Snow White settled them down. "Hold your applause, please. I must admit, this was not my idea."

She called her daughter to the stage and put her arm around Apple's shoulders. "My daughter, Apple, thought bringing back Dragon Games would unite everyone with school spirit!"

Apple stared at her mother. "No, I didn't.... That's not true!"

The students were all so excited about the dragon competition that they ignored Apple's protests, shouting, "Way to go, Apple!"

Uncertain what else to do, Apple shrugged and blushed.

Snow White then announced, "But wait—there's more! Now, if you'll all follow me outside..."

The school's stables and old arena were hidden behind a curtain of bluebirds. The students gathered around while dwarves in yellow hard hats packed up their shovels and construction equipment.

"I can't very well bring back Dragon Games in an old, dilapidated arena!" Snow White put on a hard hat with her crown on top. "Allow me to present...the new *Ever After High Dragon Games Center*!"

The birds moved aside, revealing the renovated Dragon Games Center and Arena. It was beautiful, with enough bleachers for the entire school. Two sculpted dragons, one light and one dark, framed the arena. Each was holding a giant hourglass.

The students and teachers and even Milton Grimm gushed a loud "Ohhhh..." together.

Apple grabbed her mom and pulled her aside. "Wow, Mom, why didn't you tell me about all this? And why say it was my idea when it wasn't?"

Snow grinned a brilliant smile. "You're welcome, my little Apple dumpling."

"But, Mom, it's a lie," Apple insisted.

Snow replied, "You're not Cedar Wood; you are Apple White. We discussed this! A little White lie won't harm anyone. Sometimes you have to pull out all the stops and use your resources to get your fairytale back on track."

Apple was upset. "Mira was right. We are different."

"Who?" Snow asked, just as Mira stepped in front of Raven, speaking loudly so everyone would hear.

"Me," Mira said, pointing to herself. "And you can't always just buy popularity, Snow."

Everyone gasped at Mira's boldness.

"Miss Shards! Mind your manners!" Grimm warned.

Snow laughed. "'Mira Shards.' Very clever. Rumor has it you're an excellent dragon rider. For a new kid on the block."

Mira looked boldly into Snow's eyes. "The rumor's true."

Snow nodded slowly. "Only you're not a student. You might've been once—back when we were in school." She folded her arms across her royal chest. "I'd know that arched brow anywhere."

Apple gulped, knowing everything was about to be revealed.

Raven watched Mira closely—she *had* seemed so familiar. But why?

"I just wanted to be close to my daughter!" Mira announced at last. "You can understand that."

Raven let that sink in. "Daughter?" *Oh no!*

"And to be young again," Snow said, pointing out the obvious.

"You'd have done it, too, if you could." Mira's voice shook as she asked, "I suppose now you're going to send me back to that awful mirror prison?" With that, Mira raised one eyebrow super high, just as she'd done when Raven visited her in the tower.

Raven's jaw dropped in shock. *"Mom?"*

Mira spun in a whirlwind of purple smoke, morphing into her adult self—the Evil Queen.

"Sorry, birdy. Guilty as charged," Mira announced, sweeping back her royal cloak with a flourish.

"Yay! The Evil Queen's here!" Madeline Hatter cheered. Everyone stared at her uncomfortably. Maddie quickly corrected herself: "Said no one ever!"

Suddenly, everyone in Ever After High understood that Mira was the Evil Queen. People started screaming! Running! Scrambling to get away!

Raven didn't move. She stared at her mother with a look of horror and shame....

CHAPTER 8

The Evil Queen pushed her way to the podium and faced the crowd. Her eyes glowed a fiery red. The students stopped running and turned back, fearful yet curious to see what she was going to do.

Raven rushed to her mom, inserting herself between the Evil Queen and everyone else. Her hands, crackling with power, were outstretched in a protective gesture.

Her friends watched as, below the standoff, in two new dragon corrals, the twelve dragon babies were playing in the hay. Six were white, six dark. Fog settled around the arena, giving it a magical, mysterious feel.

"Stand back, Mother!" Raven kept her hands raised. "I don't know how you escaped from your prison, but I will *not* let you hurt my friends."

The red glow in the Evil Queen's eyes faded, and she

looked at Raven innocently, as if to say, *Who, me?* She no longer looked threatening.

❧

Faybelle Thorn, the daughter of the Dark Fairy, who cursed Sleeping Beauty, looked on from the stands with interest. She hadn't realized that Apple's new friend, Mira, was actually the Evil Queen. She straightened her cheerhexing skirt and flapped her little wings, thinking, *If only I'd known before now…*

❧

"Raven, I love that you're willing to fight with your magic powers, but you judge me too harshly. I don't wish harm." She transformed into Mira for a beat, then back again. "While I was posing as Mira, I got to know your friends. I'd like to think of them as *our* friends."

"Nice try, Mom. I know your tricks," Raven said.

"No tricks. I did the crime; I did the time. Daughter, it is not so hard to change." The queen then zapped Professor Rumpelstiltskin, who was sitting in the front row of the bleachers. He croaked as he became a frog, still wearing a hat. The frog jumped into Hopper Croakington II's arms.

"See. He just changed." The queen laughed as if this proved her point.

"Welcome to *my* world," Hopper, son of the Frog Prince, said to the frog.

Frog Rumpelstiltskin slipped out of Hopper's hands. He dropped straight down off the stands and into a muddy puddle.

A pair of real frogs raised their eyes out of the brown water and looked at him in a distrustful way. One of them shot its tongue out to catch a fly and knocked off Rumpelstiltskin's hat.

The Evil Queen turned to Snow White. She bowed her head and held up her wrists, waiting to be cuffed. "Snow White, I surrender to Your Queen's justice."

The crowd murmured with surprise.

Faybelle was the only one who saw the Evil Queen quickly glance in her direction. The queen was not sincere. This was getting more and more interesting to the Dark Fairy's daughter.

Two dwarves, decked out in sunglasses and wearing security earpieces, moved to apprehend the Evil Queen, but Snow stopped them with a subtle shake of her head.

"But I promise, I am reformed," the Evil Queen went on. "Raven, my child, my escape was only to get closer to you. I missed you so." With that, she grasped Raven's hands in hers.

Raven pulled away.

In a melodramatic and overblown series of gestures, the

Evil Queen turned back to face the crowd in the bleachers. She stepped down the stairs so that she was slightly below Snow.

Faybelle nearly laughed. It was all so predictable. The queen was putting on quite the show.

"I will miss all this back in my mirror prison." The Evil Queen glanced up and pretended to notice the Dragon Games gear for the first time. "And now you have dragons. Why, what fun we could have had together playing Dragon Games."

"No more games, Mother," Raven said firmly.

The Evil Queen looked up at Snow. "Remember, Snow?"

"I remember...." Snow White said. There was a competitive gleam in her eye. "It was our game. What a rivalry." She reached her hand out toward the Evil Queen, for a moment forgetting where they were. "You against me, on our dragons. It hexcited the whole school, the whole realm...."

"And united it." The Evil Queen jumped off the podium and landed firmly in the corral area. She looked back up at Snow and the crowd of students and teachers watching from the bleachers. She slowly rotated, taking in the arena.

"The love of the sport," she said with passion. "Dragon Games were the one thing that kept my mind off trying to rule the world...." The Evil Queen suddenly lit up, as if a brand-new idea had just taken form. "Say, I could coach a team if I wasn't sent back into the mirror. What do you say, Snow White? Feel up to a rematch?" The Evil Queen rushed back up the stone steps, coming eye-to-eye with Snow White at the podium. "Or is the 'Fairest of Them All' afraid of a little competition?"

Snow paused, clearly thinking about the challenge. No one dared to breathe. "Ha!" she said at last. "If I recall, the crowds were cheering for me." She poked the Evil Queen in the shoulder. "Okay, you're on," she said. "You won't 'snow' what hit you!"

The crowd gasped in shock, but it was Raven who was the most surprised.

"I hereby grant the Evil Queen a temporary pardon," Snow announced. Then she told a dwarf, "Have the paperwork drawn up, AESOP."

Raven knew she had to stop this. She rushed forward, stepping between the queens. She said to Snow White, "*What!* No! With all due respect, Your Majesty, how can you trust my mom not to be *evil* when she just turned a teacher into a frog?"

"That? Evil?" The Evil Queen laughed. "Oh, come on! Okay, I'm changing him back.... Ya happy?" She zapped a spell into the corral toward the puddle.

She missed Professor Rumpelstiltskin, hitting another frog with her power and creating a clone of the teacher. This new Rumpelstiltskin checked himself, surprised to find he had a human body now.

"*Ribbit.*" The real Rumpelstiltskin hopped around in protest, but no one noticed.

"Happy?" The queen pointed at the fake Rumpelstiltskin.

"I'll be happy when you do something good that's not part of some bargain. Find me when you do." Raven hurried down the stairs into the corral. She moved quickly into the dragon stables and disappeared from view.

"Really, Raven," the Evil Queen shouted after her daughter. "For a girl rejecting her dark side, you've got to lighten up."

"Raven, wait!" Apple was about to follow, but Snow held her back. She said to the Evil Queen, "I'm sure your daughter will come around. Evil is relative, after all." Snow then took the Evil Queen's hand and raised it triumphantly. Together, they moved toward the magnificent dragon sculpture and then separated. Snow White went to stand by the light dragon, while the Evil Queen stood by the dark one.

Snow White announced to the students in the stands, "We two queens will be your coaches. It will take many months of hard training for these young dragons to be large enough for full-contact play, but we must begin practices immediately. Tomorrow, bright and early, we will choose our captains and teams. Let us begin a new era of *Dragon Games*!"

Having finished her speech, Snow White leaned over to one of her bodyguard dwarves standing beneath the sculpture. "Get my merchandising team working on this."

When no one was looking at her, the Evil Queen quickly zapped the muddy puddle. She smiled as a frog, the real Rumpelstiltskin, levitated from the puddle and landed in her pocket.

Time for a breaking-news story via MirrorCast.

"And there you have it, subscrollers." Blondie Lockes smiled for her audience. "Dragon Games are *back*! Hex yeah!"

CHAPTER 9

Snow and Apple got into the royal pumpkin stretch carriage. The instant the dwarf chauffeur closed the door, Apple blurted out, "A pardon? Why?"

"Don't fret, Applesauce!" Snow said. There were refreshments in the carriage. Next to a tower of pastries was a bowl of walnuts. She cracked one and ate it. "Why would anyone allow evil to roam free? That is, without a backup plan..."

"Um, sure...I knew that." Apple felt better knowing her mom had a plan.

"I have a secret weapon: Behold the Booking Glass," Snow told Apple. She held up an ornate mirror, the handle encrusted with jewels that doubled as buttons. "This has magic that can return the Evil Queen to the mirror prison forever after." She glanced at her own reflection in the Booking Glass.

Snow pressed one long, manicured finger on a ruby-red jewel, activating the magic mirror. It glowed around the rim with light magic.

Snow pointed the mirror at the bowl of walnuts and commanded, "Capture walnuts!"

"Capturing walnuts," Mirrie said with a series of beeps before it sucked the bowl of walnuts up and into the glass.

"Fairy good, Mirrie! Technology is so hexciting these days." Snow grinned at Apple. "So...if the Evil Queen is truly reformed—yeah, unlikely—my pardon makes me look just and pure."

Apple asked, "And if she is still evil?"

"I'll use this to recapture her." Snow raised the mirror and looked at herself in the glass. "I'll be a heroine! More glory for me. It's a win-win, Apple strudel."

At the new dragon stables, Daring was making sure that his hair was perfect, that his teeth sparkled white, and that his eyes didn't look too tired, while Holly and Poppy looked after the dragons. He stared in his handheld mirror. The jewels on the handle glittered in the daylight as he turned to the left to check his own profile image.

Wham. One of the dragons he was training lost control during his first flight. His tail wildly smacked the mirror out of Daring's hand. Daring rushed forward and cradled his precious mirror gently. The glass was cracked.

Setting aside the broken mirror, Daring flipped back his perfect hair. He said, "Hey, little guy, that's seven years' bad luck—which I guess isn't long in dragon years. Lucky for me, mirrors are cheap, and I buy in bulk." He grabbed a new one from his pack, leaving behind about ten more spares.

They were all identical to Snow's Booking Glass....

CHAPTER 10

Raven was at her locker when Ashlynn asked her, "Are you going to join the team tomorrow?"

"No," Raven replied, grabbing her books for class. "My mother is up to something, Ashlynn. I just can't believe that this isn't part of some evil plan. I don't want to get involved."

A few lockers down, Faybelle silently watched the exchange. Fluttering her wings, she rose from the ground and disappeared around the corner—the opposite way Raven was headed.

The Dragon Games Center was not just amazing new stables and glittering stands; there was a gorgeous office center, too. The interior of the building was like a fancy skybox:

Glass windows faced the field far below. Golden balls sat on racks against the wall. Whiteboards for the coaches showed *x*'s and *o*'s in complicated Dragon Games play patterns.

Shelves were heavy with old trophies of various shapes and heights, and along the walls were faded pictures showing team photos of the past. Beyond the hall of memories were large columns supporting a viewing balcony. The center had everything a Dragon Games coach could ever want, and more.

The Evil Queen settled into her office and arranged her desk to have a full view of the arena. She set a large glass jar on the shelf. Inside was the frog version of Professor Rumpelstiltskin. On another shelf was a small, stylized terrarium that held other creatures: newts, salamanders, spiders, snails.

The queen was at her desk when Faybelle knocked on the door. "Enter if you dare...." Raising her head slightly, the Evil Queen looked sternly at the newcomer. "Faybelle Thorn. To what do I owe the honor of a visit from the Dark Fairy's daughter?"

Faybelle fluttered forward. "You are, like, a legend! So wicked!" She spoke with a mix of genuine hero worship and fawning.

"I've changed.... Didn't you hear?" the queen assured her.

Faybelle leaned in and studied the queen's face. "Yeah, *riiiight*. Anyway. A girl could learn a lot from someone as intelligent, beautiful, smart, powerful..." She piled on the compliments.

"Got it. What do you want? Spit it out. The truth." With

a zap from the Evil Queen's finger, a spell touched Faybelle's lips.

Overcome by magic, she blurted out her story. "The truth: Nobody pays enough attention to me. I want popularity, power, and respect! I want to be like you!" She seemed surprised that she was saying all this. "Make me your Dragon Games captain. I was listening to Raven, and she said that there is no way she's going to be on your team."

The queen put a hand over her heart. "Raven said that?"

Faybelle nodded, then told the queen, "I would do anything—anything—to be like you."

"Anything? Hmm, okay, I believe you may be of use to me." A quick wave of her hand, and Faybelle snapped out of the spell. The Evil Queen moved toward her shelf of critters. She tapped on the jar containing Frog Rumpelstiltskin, tipping the lid to allow his croaks to bust out.

It took only a second for Faybelle to understand.

"Let me share a bit of my dark magic with you. There are many teachers here who do not trust me," the queen whispered. "Here is what you need to do...." As she spoke, Faybelle's eyes turned dark, and her lips curled into an evil grin.

That evening, Raven went down to the stables with Nevermore. "Now, Nevermore, it's time for you to sleep in the stables with the other dragons. Don't worry. I'll be back in the morning."

While getting Nevermore ready for sleep, Raven looked around the new space.

Baby dragons, light and dark, were separated into two different sleeping areas. Holly, Poppy, and Briar were snoozing on cushiony piles of hay, completely passed out after an exhausting day. Dragons were scattered around them, sleeping in awkward poses, some snoring loudly.

"A lot of hexcitement around here, huh, girl?" Raven asked her dragon. "Might be pretty strange for a while, you know, while my mom is here." She rubbed Nevermore's belly and scratched her neck.

From the shadows behind a pillar, the Evil Queen made a magical gesture, causing Nevermore to yawn and immediately fall fast asleep. Raven yawned, too. She closed her eyes, muttering, "My mom *never* apologizes or is sweet. Who is that woman?" She could barely keep her eyes open. "So tired! Maybe I'll just sleep out here with you tonight." She looped an arm over Nevermore and relaxed into the hay.

The shadow of the Evil Queen loomed over the stables. Her eyes gleamed in the darkness as she walked slowly toward the school.

CHAPTER 11

Raven was awoken by the call of a rooster. She stretched and sat up, only to discover it wasn't really a rooster, but rather one of the baby dragons crowing. She reached out to the hay beside her. "Good morning, Nevermore...." Her dragon wasn't there. "Nevermore? Where are you?"

Raven checked in the stable stall where Holly and Poppy kept the babies. Nevermore wasn't there. "Nevermore!" Something was wrong.... She dashed out of the stables and into the school. *"Nevermore?"*

Raven searched the library. *"Nevermore? Here, dragon, dragon!"* No dragon, but Raven was getting an idea of where to look. "Oh, I bet she has you!" she told herself.

The Evil Step-Librarians gave her a warning. *"Huuuuu-sshhhhhhhh!"*

Raven didn't hang around. She hurried out of the library

and didn't see that, immediately after she left, Faybelle appeared from behind a bookshelf with an empty jar in one hand. She used the Evil Queen's magic to turn the Evil Step-Librarians into snails and exchange them with real snails in librarian form.

Faybelle smiled at the real Evil Step-Librarians through the glass before sealing the lid tightly and warning them, "Shhhhh."

At the Dragon Games Arena, Snow White stood next to the Evil Queen. In front of them was a line of students. Twin corrals, to the left and right of the bleachers, contained all the young dragons. Dark dragons were on one side and light dragons on the other. Some babies were sleeping; others were playing. None of them were ready to fly, but a few were fluttering around, desperately trying.

"First will be the choosing of the two teams and captains," Headmaster Milton Grimm announced to the gathered students. "Following that, since your dragons are not fledged—"

"It will be many a patient month before they are full-sized," his brother Giles interrupted.

"Ah yes, months," Milton echoed what his brother was saying. "Today you will merely walk your young dragons through their paces."

The students were disappointed.

Giles told them, "But no fear! The Evil Queen will today offer a master-class demonstration of dragon riding."

Before turning over the microphone to the Evil Queen, Milton warned, "Now, this can be a very dangerous sport, and it is of vital importance that you understand and follow all the rules."

Most of the students nodded in agreement. In the last row of the bleachers, Faybelle Thorn booed.

Giles held up a coin, black on one side and white on the other. He flipped it without seeing the purple spark that hit the coin before it reached the ground.

"Dark wins," he said. "Your Majesty, you may choose first."

The Evil Queen grinned. "I choose Apple White as my dark captain."

"What?" Apple protested. "But I should be on Team Light, my mom's team...."

"I object!" Snow moved quickly in from the side of the light dragon sculpture. From behind her back, she began to pull out the Booking Glass mirror.

The Evil Queen said, "Oh, Snow, bending the rules? *Tsk-tsk*. We have not even begun to play the real game."

Snow hesitated, lowering the Booking Glass slightly.

Feeling trapped and unsure what to do, Apple stood between the queens.

"Apple, be a sport." The Evil Queen reached out and took Apple's hand. "Join the dark." She lowered her voice and whispered, "Let me tell you a little story: When I was released from my mirror prison, I could only—"

"*No!*" Apple shrieked, fearful that the Evil Queen was

going to tell the secret of who had released her. She groaned sadly. "I mean, yes, I'll be on your team." Turning to her mom, Apple said, "It's just a game, right? Let's mix it up. Your turn, Mom!" With another groan, she stepped behind the Evil Queen and took her place on Team Dark.

Snow reined in her emotions, smiling as she said, "I choose Darling Charming as captain of the Light Team."

Milton Grimm then announced, "Captains, choose your teams! You may each select three players."

Apple considered the options. "I choose..." She paused. The Evil Queen told her whom to pick. "Ashlynn Ella, Melody Piper, and Madeline Hatter," Apple said loudly.

Maddie wasn't in the stands. She was with her cotton-candy-blowing dragon in the corral. The dragon blew pink cotton candy onto Maddie's head, making a fancy bouffant wig. Maddie adjusted it, then said, "Ready!"

As the Dark Team gathered, the Evil Queen called Faybelle over and gave her instructions. Faybelle nodded, flying up toward the school tower.

Darling selected Team Light. "I choose Poppy O'Hair, Holly O'Hair, and Raven Queen."

The crowd gasped, then cheered. Raven walked up the stairs, where she could easily see down into the dragon corrals. Her eyes scanned for Nevermore. Where was she?

Raven told Darling, "Whoa. I'm not here to join up." She pinned her eyes on her mother. "Mom, did you take Nevermore?"

"She is fine." The Evil Queen glanced up at the tower

above the school before telling Raven, "Mummy has taken care of everything. Now, we have one more pick."

"If not Raven…Lizzie Hearts," Darling said.

Over the shouts from the crowd, Raven demanded, "Mom! Where is Nevermore?"

The Evil Queen gave Raven an evil smile and said, "Dragons are meant to be ridden."

In the highest turret above the school, Nevermore was chained to the railing. She roared, thrashed, and pulled at the chains, desperate to escape.

The noise brought attention from the stands.

Raven looked at her dragon, then glared at her mom. "What the hex?"

In the tower, Faybelle saddled Nevermore and climbed on, just as she'd been told.

The instant she removed the chains, the dragon took off, dragging Faybelle through the air. She could barely hold on. They zigged and zagged above the bleachers as Nevermore tried to toss off Faybelle and return to Raven.

"*Aaaaaaaaaaaaaaaaaaahhhhhhh!*" Faybelle screamed.

The Evil Queen acted as if this was all quite boring.

The queen did a presto chango, revealing riding pants underneath her dress. It was a fabulous moment, and the queen took in the applause as she leaped into Nevermore's saddle. Before taking off, she told Faybelle, "This is all a distraction. Fetch me Snow's magic mirror. I need that Booking Glass!"

"Right! Spella good idea!" Faybelle said.

"Hyah!" The Evil Queen gave Nevermore a kick, and the dragon rose into the air. She did a few tricks, a spiral, and a loop to rally the crowd.

Snow White was annoyed, but she used the opportunity. She spoke into the microphone, her voice booming through the arena. "Ahem. Focus! Students, Dragon Games are very beautiful and very fun, but they can also be very dangerous. Let's fly through the rules." She enjoyed a good pun.

"The game is played in two periods." The Evil Queen soared by the hourglasses by each dragon statue on Nevermore, pointing out where to look while Snow said, "As you can see, the hourglasses keep the time. The Dark and Light Teams will take turns attempting to score."

The big screen at one end of the arena lit up and showed old videos of the game.

Snow White went on. "There are three players on the field for each team. Six dragon riders total. Each team has one defensive player, one offensive. The third teammate can travel anywhere on the field but cannot score. The ball is lobbed into play, and the dragon rider must catch the ball and fly it through a hooped goalpost to score."

The Evil Queen zoomed from a light goal hoop on one side to a dark one on the other.

"The goalposts normally would be high in the air, but

because these dragons are just hatchlings, they've been lowered to ground level." That was it. "Any questions?"

All future riders raised their hands.

Snow pointed at Poppy first. "If you're playing the forewand position, can you pass the orb to your swooper?"

Holly jumped in with, "Can you score on both nesters or only the opposing team's?"

The Evil Queen flew down near Snow. She winked and said, "Perhaps it would be clearer if you joined me?"

Snow turned to face the crowd, offering a small smile and mild protest. "Now? Oh, I couldn't. It's been ages." She pretended to resist for a beat while the crowd called her name, louder and louder, until finally she gave in. "Well, if you insist. Got to give the people what they want!"

Snow pulled off her outer skirt, revealing her own dragon-riding gear. A loud whistle summoned Legend to her. She flew into the arena. No one was surprised to see her wearing a saddle.

Blondie Lockes was immediately on the air, reporting the news.

"Ooh, this is fairy hexciting! Dragon Games are happening, people! Spread the word...."

CHAPTER 12

Launchers set up giant, holographic gemstone curtains into the air. Among the diamonds was a ruby, worth many more points. The goal was to touch a golden ball to the gems and change the ball's value. Points were only given when that golden ball made it through the goalpost hoops at either side of the majestic arena.

A whistle blew and the golden ball shot up over the arena.

The two queens raced for it.

Snow maneuvered early and caught the ball first. She was flying toward the glowing ruby when she was sidechecked by the Evil Queen. The ball was knocked out of her hands and fell toward the ground.

Both riders zoomed in, and the Evil Queen caught it on a rebound. She spun Nevermore around and headed back toward the opposite goal.

Snow blocked her. "You've kept fit in mirror prison," she said. "I'm impressed."

The Evil Queen moved left, then right. "It's nice to see you on a dragon for once, instead of your high horse."

The pair zoomed past the crowd. Students filmed the air show on their MirrorPhones and MirrorPads.

Faybelle sneaked up behind the dwarf standing guard over Snow White's purse. He was distracted, looking up at the game. She started to pickpocket the Booking Glass from the slightly open bag, but she was interrupted by Daring Charming. Acting innocent, she sat abruptly on the bench next to Snow's purse.

Daring put his backpack down and joined her. The two bags were side by side on the ground, sitting between Daring and Faybelle.

"I haven't seen a vision this spellbinding since I last checked my hair. Speaking of which—" He reached in his bag and pulled out one of his hand mirrors to check his reflection. His bag flopped open, and another mirror tilted out. "Just as I suspected—still perfect!" He flipped back his bangs and put his mirror down on the bench.

Faybelle held back a grin as she took his fake mirror and traded it for Snow White's Booking Glass. "Excuse me, Daring. Gotta go. The, uh..." She looked him over and said, "The glare from your smile is blinding my view." She had Snow White's mirror and was off!

"I'm so handsome it's almost a curse," Daring said, waving as she stood to go. Just then, Snow White and the Evil Queen buzzed over the crowd. The backdraft knocked Faybelle over. She stumbled and dropped the mirror.

Daring helped her up. His foot bumped his bag and a third, identical mirror fell onto the ground. The real Booking Glass slid under the seats.

Daring picked up the fake mirror and handed it to Faybelle, saying, "You dropped this! Nice taste in mirrors, by the way." He smiled, then stopped, curling his lips over his teeth. "Sorry, are you blinded?"

Faybelle shook her head, then grabbed the mirror and hurried away. Daring went to zip his backpack and found the other mirror beneath the seats. He spun it in his hands, but it looked exactly like the others. "Or was this her mirror?" he muttered. "Oh well, I have plenty! No matter…" He took a look at his reflection. "It's what's in it that counts!"

The Evil Queen paused in midair. She looked around and found Faybelle signaling her with glints of light reflected by the mirror. The Evil Queen nodded, reined in Nevermore, and, with a fancy flourish, landed by the podium. The crowd went wild!

Nevermore finally shook off Faybelle's spell and shrank to dog size. She flew fast and furious, away from the Evil Queen and to Raven in the front row of the bleachers.

Daring sat down beside her. "Raven, I hate to say it, but your mom is kind of wicked amazing."

Raven hugged Nevermore. "You're half right."

Snow landed her dragon directly on the sculpture of the light dragon. She gave Legend a little treat and then let her go off on her own.

"The teams will now take the field!" She rotated the giant hourglass above the dugout of her team.

The gates to the two dragon corrals opened, and the players marched out, leading the baby dragons on leashes. Some came along nicely, but others tugged back and had to be almost dragged along.

Sparrow Hood looked at the babies and, after the amazing show they'd just seen, shouted, "Boring! More queens!"

His voice was drowned out when the golden ball was fired into the air and holographic gems rose again. This time, the entire setup was merely a few inches above the ground.

Apple bounded forward, leading her baby dragon. Hers was the only light dragon on the Dark Team and was the best behaved of them all.

The ball rolled across the field. Apple's dragon picked up the golden ball and looked up at her expectantly.

Sparrow changed his mind, saying, "Okay, this is adorable! *Ooooooooooh!*"

"Do we get hextra points if our dragons are hextra cute?" Holly asked as the golden ball rolled in front of her. Her dragon jumped behind her leg, afraid of the ball.

Raven shook her head. This was one big, terrible day. She carried Nevermore out of the stands and down the stone steps into the corral, where there was a tunnel that went to the stables.

"Come on, Nevermore," Raven said. "Let's get you taken care of."

The Evil Queen noticed Raven leaving and gestured for Faybelle to follow.

In the dragon stables, Raven tugged on a rope that opened a chute in the ceiling. Dragon chow flowed down into a communal dragon feeding trough.

"I don't get you, Raven Queen.... If my mom were as wicked cool as yours," Faybelle said, entering the stable, "I would do anything to be ruling at her side."

Raven replied, "That's how we're different, Faybelle. I won't do anything to please her. Especially not if it means my friends could get hurt."

The two girls walked through the stables, the long food trough like a barrier between them. Faybelle secretly sprinkled a magic powder in the trough, coating the dragon's food.

Nevermore finished eating, and Raven settled her dragon into her stall.

Faybelle looked at the food trough. The powder glittered with evil magic on the nuggets of chow. She smiled. Nevermore hadn't eaten the charmed food, but the others surely would.

CHAPTER 13

Above the stables at the arena, the last grains of sand poured into the bottom of an hourglass. A buzzer sounded.

Over the whoops from the stands, Snow announced, "That's it for the first half! Dragon riders, please take your beasts to the stables for refreshment."

The players led their baby dragons down through the corrals and into the tunnels beneath the central bleachers. The baby dragons poked their heads into the food trough and started gobbling their meal.

Faybelle watched nearby. She called the Evil Queen on her MirrorPhone.

"The eagle has landed...." Faybelle said when the queen picked up.

The queen had no clue what that meant. "Eagle? What

eagle? What about the dragons? Did you feed them the growth formula?"

Faybelle peeked over her shoulder to see that the baby dragons were, in fact, growing! Oddly, not all their parts were growing at the same rate.... The girls in the stables gasped as some dragons suddenly had very long necks. Others, long legs. One got a very, very long tail.

Faybelle started to explain, "It was code—I—" Then she said, "Never mind. Yes."

The formula worked!

"Hexcellent," the Evil Queen said with a chuckle. "Then it is going to be a wild and wicked second half of the game."

Snow stood at the top of the arena stairs between the corrals. "Time for round two!" she declared. "My subjects, trust your queen—if you think Dragon Games are exciting when the dragons are just babies, just you wait until they are big and—" The cheers of the crowd cut her off.

From the tunnels, full-sized dragons emerged with their riders on their backs! They moved past Snow White and onto the playing field.

Snow flipped around to look at the Evil Queen.

"What?" The Evil Queen looked back at her blankly. "Don't look at me! I was right here the whole time!"

The students shouted, "*Woo!* Look at the size of them!"

"Magic rocks!"

"Whoever did this, we love you!"

"Mega dragon party!"

Snow looked nervous. Her two bodyguard dwarves came in for instructions.

As she leaned in to talk to them, the Evil Queen leaned in to listen.

"This is the work of powerful magic. We have to stop the game. These riders won't be able to handle full-sized dragons...." Snow started.

The Evil Queen stepped forward and threw Snow's original words back at her. "What happened to 'give the people what they want'?"

Snow listened to the crowd's thunderous applause. Finally, she gave in. Taking the microphone from a dwarf, she announced, "You want Dragon Games? Here comes the second half of the game—bigger, better..."

Under her breath, the Evil Queen added, "And badder..."

Snow White instead said, "...and about to begin!"

The Evil Queen reached up to flip over the timekeeping hourglass. The buzzer sounded to mark the beginning of the second half.

The now-larger dragons began flapping their wings. There was a collective roar, and they lifted off, climbing higher and higher into the air.

Snow White brought her riders in for a huddle. The dragons loomed six feet above the ground in a circle around her.

"Have fun," she told them.

The riders cheered.

On the other side of the arena, the Evil Queen was in her huddle, framed by the gates of their corral. Faybelle stood beside her while Apple, Ashlynn, Maddie, and Melody hovered on dragonback.

"This isn't just a game. You are to win by any means necessary," the Evil Queen instructed her team.

"Huh?" Ashlynn replied.

The Evil Queen ignored her. "Victory is all that matters. Take your positions!"

The Light and Dark Teams hovered high over the field, facing each other. Two dragons were at the midfield line; one held back at the goal area. Apple's dragon was snapping at Darling's dragon.

Fairies on the scoreboard loaded zero cards for each side.

At the buzzer, the golden ball was launched into the air, and holographic jewels rose up from the ground, creating gemstone barriers at various places around the field.

The golden ball began to fall, when Melody zoomed ahead of Lizzie to grab it. She whispered into her dragon's ear, and the dragon soared toward the midline, where Apple swooped in to receive the pass!

"Great catch!" Melody said. "Go for the ruby!"

Apple moved quickly and tagged it against the ruby, rubifying the ball. She dodged Darling's dragon and—*wham*—Apple scored a goal!

The crowd cheered for the Dark Team!

More jewels shot up like a beaded curtain. One of the glittering jewels was blood-red. As Apple directed her dragon through it, the golden ball changed to a deep red.

"That's worth ten points if I can get it in the goal!" she told herself.

Game on!

Glowing with the red ball's light, Apple took off toward the Light Team's hoop. She was about to score a goal when Darling sneaked up and grabbed the ball from her.

"Go, Darling!" Raven shouted from the stands.

Ashlynn and Melody closed in around Darling, trying to stop her. Lizzie broke in from behind. Darling tossed her the ball, and Lizzie touched it to a blue gem.

Darling took back the ball and was heading straight for the Dark Team's goal. Apple glanced down and caught the Evil Queen's eye. The queen nodded. Her expression told Apple to do anything to get that ball. Apple frowned but then rammed her dragon into Darling's.

"Whoaaa!" Darling's dragon spun upside down, knocking off Darling. She was close to the ground but fell hard and skidded across the grass.

"Ooooh!" The crowd watched her go.

When Darling finally stopped, she held her ankle and waved for a medic. Coach Gingerbreadman whistled. "Time out!"

The medics took Darling off the field on a stretcher. Apple swooped down and hovered near the dark dragon sculpture, where the Evil Queen was waiting for her.

"People are getting hurt! My friends!" Apple said, bringing her dragon in close enough for the conversation to be private.

"A necessary evil," the queen said simply. "Remember, we must get Raven to take the field for the plan to work!"

"You mean I get my Happily Ever After? You promised!" Apple reminded.

"What?" She seemed to have forgotten all about that, but then she said, "Oh yes."

Apple accepted that and flew back to the game, ready to play.

⟶

Snow White and the school nurse leaned over Darling.

"I'm good, Coach. Put me back in."

The nurse refused to consider her request. "No."

"No?" Snow pressed her lips together. "We don't have enough players. It's over. We must forfeit the game to the Dark Team."

The nurse put an ice pack on Darling's ankle while Snow waved the rest of her team to a landing.

⟶

"What's happening?" Raven asked Maddie, who was in the stands instead of in the game.

"Snow White is surrendering. Your mom will win...."

The narrators told me so," Maddie said, licking cotton candy off her fingers.

"She always wins! How does she always get her way? Someone's got to be able to stop her!" Raven was mad.

"Yay! Ooh, ohh! I know this one...." Maddie thought it was a quiz. She answered, "You."

Back on the field, Snow approached the Evil Queen. "Because we do not have enough players to take the field, we surrender."

Raven arrived just then, saying, "Light will have to play with a new rider!"

She was on Nevermore, dressed and ready.

"All according to plan." The Evil Queen snickered.

CHAPTER 14

Daring was sitting comfortably in the stands, gazing into the Booking Glass. Next to him was his afternoon snack of cotton candy, popcorn, soda, and a hot dog. He pulled out a napkin from his backpack, and as he wrapped it around his neck, he noticed that the jewels on the mirror's handle really shone in the light. "Oooh, these faux gems look so real," he said. "They could use a polish, though."

He took the napkin and began rubbing the gems, accidentally hitting the pattern that opened Mirrie and unlocked the mirror's power. Not noticing the start-up chimes, he put the mirror down by his food and rubbed his hands together in hungry anticipation.

"Rapture! A delicious meal," Daring said, licking his lips.

The mirror flashed magic, which struck the meal next to him as he leaned over to get another napkin out of his backpack.

Raven Queen has finally begun to master her magical powers. But instead of using her powers for evil, Raven uses them to help her friends.

The Evil Queen does her best to trick Raven into helping her escape from mirror prison. But Raven doesn't fall for it!

Nevermore is spooked by the Evil Queen and ends up with a messy makeover. Grooming Nevermore sounds like a job for Holly and Poppy O'Hair!

After speaking with her mother, Apple White is worried about her Happily Ever After. The Evil Queen takes advantage and tricks Apple into helping her escape from mirror prison.

Meet Mira Shards—the
Evil Queen disguised
as the newest student at
Ever After High!

Raven uses magic to help the dragon eggs hatch—but Mira Shards interferes with her spell. The baby dragons are adorable! But are the dark dragons EVIL?

Dragonsport is back!
Let the Dragon Games begin!

The Evil Queen wants to take over Ever After High. Can Raven stop her mother's wicked quest?

"Capturing delicious meal." Mirrie beeped.

Daring didn't hear it. When he turned around, he exclaimed, "Oh, come on! Who took my cotton candy?"

His snack had been sent to the mirror prison.

The golden ball shot over the field. Raven grabbed it first, but Apple stole it. The ball went back and forth a few times through the floating, glowing jewels, which changed the color and point potential of the ball.

"Apple, it's just us," Raven said when they were alone.

"It's our destiny, you against me," Apple said. "Doesn't this feel right?"

"Right? My mom is free, and Darling is hurt, Apple," Raven said.

Apple had to agree. "I know. That wasn't supposed to happen. For real. But don't you want vengeance? Doesn't your heart desire victory over me? Aren't you angry?"

Raven gritted her teeth and clenched her fist. "Am I angry? Yeah, I am angry, Apple!"

"Good, follow your destiny!" Apple encouraged.

"I am angry that you don't listen. I am angry that you say you're my friend but are so…selfish. It's all about what you want. What kind of friend refuses to listen?" Raven asked.

Apple felt teary. "I…I…just want our Happily Ever After."

Raven passed Apple the ball. "Have it, be a winner, but I'm out. I am not playing any games anymore. All yours."

With a swift tug on Nevermore's reins, she headed down to the corral.

"At least my mom will be proud of me!" Apple shouted to Raven before she charged to the goal and scored.

The crowd went crazy while the scorekeeper fairies loaded a thousand points on the Dark Team's side of the board.

Apple flew straight to the Evil Queen. "It won't work! Raven won't turn evil!"

"She doesn't have to. You see, that is the beauty. It is enough that others think she has. Head back in. I got this."

When no one was looking, the Evil Queen cast a spell on Nevermore. *"A smoldering pyre to a dragon flier, I summon forth uncontrollable fire!"*

Raven flew Nevermore toward the school tower. "What has my mom done to Apple? How can she think—*whoa!*" Raven was concerned as Nevermore burped a rocket-engine blast of blue flame. When the dragon burped again, there was another shot of fire.

"Look! It's Raven. Since she's such a sore loser, she's taking revenge by burning down the school!" Faybelle shouted, pointing.

With a big belch, Nevermore accidentally ignited the ivy on the outer wall of the school. Flames began to billow.

"Nevermore! No!" Raven took the dragon down toward the arena, where another wild burp set the roof of the stables on fire.

"You!" Snow White accused the Evil Queen. "You are up to your wicked ways again!"

"Me? She's on your team! I've learned that she is the one who made the dragons grow so big! Was that irresponsible act on your orders, too?" The Evil Queen shook her head in horror.

Snow was done! She whipped the magic mirror out of her purse and hit the jewels in the secret order. "Wake up, Mirrie! Capture the Evil Queen!"

Nothing.

Snow White smacked it against her hand. The cheap imitation mirror broke apart.

"Oh, were you looking for this?" The Evil Queen tapped the jewels on her own mirror. It also broke apart.

⟩⟩

Daring saw the queens with their mirrors and said to himself, "Hey, I have one of those, too. Only mine is shinier. It captures my best side." He rubbed the handle with his sleeve, accidentally pressing the jewels in the correct order and activating the mirror again. He gazed at himself in the glass, transfixed as usual. "Perhaps I should have my portrait done.... It would take quite the artiste to capture Daring Charming."

"Capturing Daring Charming," Mirrie said with a few beeps.

A second later, Daring vanished. The mirror fell to the ground.

"Cool!" Daring said from inside the glass. "A world of mirrors! Hey..." He looked all around. "Why can't I see myself? I'm on the flipside of the mirrors? Nooooo." But then he saw something that made him happy. "Oooh! My cotton candy!"

"The games are over. Take her," the Evil Queen instructed her fake animal faculty to apprehend Snow White.

Raven watched her mother from the smoldering tower. "She did it! She took control of the entire school! What's next?"

CHAPTER 15

The Evil Queen took the podium. "In this time of trouble, a strong leader is needed. I humbly request the keys to power, temporarily, so I can restore order to this chaos and bring whoever else is responsible for these crimes to justice. Even if it is my own daughter." She eyed the crowd. "Do you accept?"

"Yyyyyyuuuuurrrrp." The fake Milton Grimm handed the Evil Queen the big ceremonial keys to the school.

Book End breaking news! Blondie Lockes, reporting live at what's left of the new Dragon Games Center, ever after a devastating blaze! Headmaster Grimm just handed the Evil Queen the keys to the school! She vows to catch whoever started the fire, even if that's her own daughter, Raven! The question remains: Will this new headmistress restore order to Ever After High, her being the Evil Queen and all? Let's cut to the arena for her statement...."

The Evil Queen stood on a platform, front and center with the fake Milton Grimm before the rowdy arena crowd. "Students, don't get over-hexcited! I am but a temporary substitute. Milton Grimm will resume leadership as headmaster as soon as this crisis is over...."

"*Ribbit*," Milton Grimm agreed.

The queen grinned. "He has a frog in his throat."

As the students debated this turn of events, a crazed dark dragon broke free and charged the crowd like a bull. The group panicked and started to scatter. The Evil Queen shot a lasso of light that whirled around the dragon, calming it.

"Dark dragon, heel! Stay calm!" She told the crowd, "See? Trust Headmistress Queenie. Everything's under control. Citizens, students—as you were! Nothing to see here!"

Everyone began to leave the arena. Darling found Daring's mirror and backpack on the bleachers. She slipped the mirror into her brother's pack and took it with her.

"Daring forgot his stuff. That's odd. He never goes anywhere without a mirror." She didn't notice that Daring was trapped in the glass.

Raven took Nevermore back into the dragon stalls, which had also been singed. She said, "It's okay, Nevermore. I know you didn't mean to start that fire. You're another victim of my mom's evil magic."

Apple entered with her dragon and saw Raven there. "They're saying *you* set the fire—on purpose."

"I didn't do it on purpose!" Raven protested. "My dragon got spontaneous fire hiccups? This has *Evil Queen* written all over it!"

"Well, don't worry," Apple assured her. "Your mom has promised to restore order. And she's so powerful—I know she can."

Raven rolled her eyes. "Come on! Do you really believe she would? I mean...really? Really?"

Apple said, "You should give your mom another chance! You're all about changing your story, Raven." She looked seriously at Raven. "Your mom broke out of that mirror prison and literally walked over *broken glass*, just to be with you!"

Raven squinted. "How could you know that?"

She stared at Apple. "It was you? You released my mother?"

Apple sniffed. "She promised me my Happily Ever After. Not just for me, but for you, too. For all of us! You've got to admit, she has been a great Dragon Games coach. And she fixed the fire damage....She's changed, Raven!"

Raven couldn't believe it. "No, Apple. *You've* changed. We are so not on the same page anymore....In fact, I don't even think we're in the same fairytale. I hope you find your

Happily Ever After, Apple. I really do. But first you'd better find a new roommate." Raven turned to leave.

Apple caught her arm. "But we were supposed to be friends forever after!"

"That's not how the story goes, Apple. Not this chapter, anyway. You can't be on both sides. Good or evil: Pick one." Raven pulled back.

Without saying anything else, Raven stormed off.

Apple was heartbroken. She took out her MirrorPhone and dialed her mom.

"This is Snow White…." the machine answered. "I'm out of the castle, but I'll get back to you as soon as I'm free."

The Evil Queen had Snow White trapped in ropelike beams of purple light.

When Apple called, Snow strained against her binds. "Let me free! Let me speak to my daughter!"

"You've said plenty, Snowball," the queen said, turning off the phone. She imitated Snow: *"Lock up the Evil Queen, let the Evil Queen be on probation."* She snorted. "It's always your way." She imitated her again. *"Oh, I'm Snow White, I'm the Fairest One of All!"* The queen was sick of Snow. *"Ha!* More like *un-*fairest."

"The magical binding is a bit overkill. Even for you." Snow surveyed the fake teachers, who were all standing behind the queen. "And what you've done to the staff is unforgivable! Switching their minds with creatures'—it's…beastly!"

"Would you be more comfortable in mirror prison, Your *Majesty*? Let me tell you from experience: You would not! Years of solitude—watching the world go by through a one-way mirrored glass. Watching your own daughter grow up without you. Or perhaps you'd rather join your beloved school staff in here?" She dipped her hand into a terrarium where she'd stashed the faculty amphibians, Salamander Giles Grimm, Blue Frog Milton Grimm, Mouse Baba Yaga, Frog Rumpelstiltskin, and the Snail Evil Step-Librarians.

The Evil Queen laughed. "This is *my* school now." She moved close to Snow. "I know your game. Bringing back the Dragon Games Center…You were going to wait till I made the slightest misstep, then lock me up again to remind everyone you're such a *perfect* queen. Well, you'll have to think quick, *Slow* White, because I have the upper hand now."

Snow stared deep into those evil eyes. "Release me. My subjects won't rest until they find their true queen."

"Not if no one knows you're gone." The Evil Queen pulled a white snake from her pocket. *"Snow of white, snake of pale! Reverse two minds, from head to tail!"* With a finger flick sparking purple vapor, the Evil Queen magically traded Snow White's mind with the mind of the snake.

"You'll never get away with *hiss*!" Snow struggled as the Evil Queen set her into the terrarium with the others.

Just then, the big office double doors swung open, and Raven marched into the room.

"Raven, my daughter! How do I look in my new, high-powered office? Room for one more—what do you say? Partner? Rule the school with me!" The queen sat on an impressive black throne.

"You want me to rule Ever After High with you? Why? So I can watch you cast evil spells on my friends as soon as you're in a bad mood? No thanks!" Raven said, glancing around.

"Friends." The queen mocked her. "Ha! Let's not forget who they blamed for that fire: *you*."

"They made a mistake," Raven said.

"Nonsense. Like it or not, birdy, your royal bloodline creates *evil expectations*. I say rise to the occasion! Be an evil queen like mummy fearest. It'll be more fun than shopping together…." The Evil Queen unrolled a map and took out a quill to mark it.

Raven groaned. Her mother's plans were nothing new.

From the terrarium, voices shouted, "Raven! Run, child, get help!"

Grimm croaked, "It is us, your beloved teachers!"

Raven noticed the cage, and when her mother turned away, she winked at the creature teachers. She then changed her approach. "Mother, you've swapped the staff with creatures? How…*clever*."

The queen was surprised. "Yes, well—wait, what? A compliment?"

Raven went on. "Well, this *is* impressive. You never cease to amaze me with your powers. *Our* powers! I mean, look at them—helpless, puny. Caged. Who could stand in your way now?" She gave a small, forced grin. "You're right, Mother. You've been right all along. We both know what I need to do. Evil."

The queen was so proud. "Oh! I have dreamed of the day you'd see the dark! Like mother, like daughter. I'm so proud of you! Get your things. Let's set you up in here at my side." She whipped up a spell. *"Eye of frog and hair of otter, make a throne fit for my daughter."*

A small matching black throne appeared next to the larger one.

Later, after listening to her mom rant on and on about taking over the world, Raven got a chance to go to her locker. There were things she needed....

Darling, limping from her dragon-riding accident, came over to her. "Raven, have you seen my brother lately? Daring, not Dexter. I haven't seen him since the whole Dragon Games Center craziness."

Raven thought. "Hmm, I haven't, actually. And he's hard to miss. He's probably just getting his teeth whitened or something." As cryptically as she could, Raven asked, "Hey, Darling, let's say a *particular student* needed to hide out for a while. Where would she go?"

"If that *particular student* wanted to find a place where,

let's say, the Evil Queen couldn't reach them? I know a perfect secret place in the Enchanted Forest...." She winked. "We are talking about you, right?"

Raven slowly nodded.

"Totally. I knew that. I'll take you there on one condition: Count me in on whatever you're up to."

"Deal," Raven said. "Meet me in the stables after school. Come alone."

A couple of lockers down, Faybelle Thorn was spying on Raven and Darling. "So Raven is trying to go rogue?" she said to herself. "If I catch her trying to bail, the Evil Queen will have to take me seriously as Future Villain. Oh, Her Evilness will be ever after so impressed! *Mwa-ha-ha!*"

CHAPTER 16

*L*ooks like it's just us, Nevermore," Raven said sadly while she put a harness on her dragon.

A noise by the door made her turn.

Darling had arrived, and with her were Ashlynn, Holly, Poppy, and Maddie.

"What part of 'come alone' didn't you get?" Raven asked, but she was glad they were all there. "I guess some backup isn't a bad idea. Thanks, you guys."

"Danger is my middle name!" Maddie said. "Well, actually, it's Xylophone. Well, actually, I have forty-two middle names, but it's in there somewhere!"

Together, they walked their dragons out of the stables.

The dark dragons roared as they passed, slamming their tails into the sides of the stable.

"Um, you guys?" Ashlynn tipped her head. "These dragons are pretty angry. We'd better move...."

Poppy and Holly had an idea. They hoisted up a huge bag of dragon treats and dumped it into the pen. The dark dragons tore off the wrapping to get to the food.

"They're Candy Witch–brand Dragon Treats," Holly said. "Irresistibly sweeeet!"

Raven and her friends took off on dragonback, flying over the back walls and turrets of the school.

Fast as her wings could carry her, Faybelle rushed back to find the Evil Queen.

"Faybelle. What have you to report?" she asked.

"She ran away."

"*She did WHAT?*" The queen got up and crossed the room in big steps. "I've restrained myself because my daughter goes to this school of fools. But if she's playing hooky, I'm not playing *nice* anymore! Get me my staff!"

Faybelle asked, "Like, from the terrarium, or…?"

The queen stomped her foot. "No, my *staff* staff."

Faybelle bowed her head. "Yes, Your Evilness!"

The Evil Queen waited for Faybelle to fetch her staff, then looked at the map of Ever After on her desk. She swept the staff over it, a light glowing as she slowly traced the area around the school. When the light crossed the Enchanted Forest section, the bright purple turned blood-red.

"She's in the Enchanted Forest?" the queen asked Faybelle.

"Oh yeah," Faybelle said. "I could have told you that."

"My magic cannot permeate the Enchanted Forest!

It's too…enchanted!" The queen bit her bottom lip and frowned.

Faybelle raised a hand as if in class.

The queen called on her. "Yes, Faybelle?"

"*Fairy magic* works in the Enchanted Forest. That's my hood. I can find them and tell you where they are!"

"Now, that is how to be an evil henchman. I'm sorry—henchfairy." The queen was pleased. Raising her staff, the queen said, "If Raven is gone, I declare school is out…*for evil*!" She cast a spell.

> "*Powers of darkness and*
> *doom,*
> *Thunder with a sonic boom.*
> *Turn these halls of education*
> *Into a castle rock formation!*"

Purple lightning shot from her staff, and magic washed over the buildings and grounds, transforming Ever After High and filling it with evil! The roots of trees grew like snaking, witchy fingers—wrapping around the buildings and barring doors and windows.

"Attention, staff and students!" The Evil Queen's voice boomed over the PA system. "I have heard that Raven has abandoned Ever After High. I don't see the point in continuing this charade.…"

The school was vibrating, so the students grabbed on to whatever they could, terrified by the darkness that was engulfing them.

"All this goodness!" the queen's voice blared. "Ugh, this place was dripping with it. I've decided to make a few changes around here. Starting now…"

Suddenly a spark of purple light swept from the tree branches, turning the faculty and staff who were not yet animals into pets. Cerise Hood watched in horror as Professor Pied Piper turned into a rat. Mr. Badwolf became a wolf cub. No one was safe!

The school lifted off the ground and rose higher and higher. The queen, out on the balcony, twirled and laughed as she got closer and closer to the domination she'd planned.

The students gathered at the windows, staring down together as the Evil Queen's voice boomed again over the PA system. "Due to our recent remodel, all classes will be canceled and replaced with evil servitude."

Faybelle was thrilled. "Wow. That was a lot of pent-up evil power," she told the queen. "I'm sorry! I didn't expect Raven to saddle up and fly the dragon coop with her friends."

"Stop flapping your lips and start flapping your wings," the queen told her. "I will prepare my dark dragons for the hunt!"

CHAPTER 17

*F*lying above a clearing in the Enchanted Forest, Raven, Darling, and their friends landed their dragons. Darling climbed down and plucked a flower from a flowery shrub.

"This is no time to stop and smell the flowers, Darling," Raven told her. "I thought you knew a secret spot where we could hide?"

"I don't...." Darling said. "But *she* does." The bush shook as a pixie emerged.

"A woodland pixie!" Ashlynn exclaimed. "How hexciting! I've never seen one in person. Or, in pixie, I guess. How do you do?"

The little pixie twittered to Ashlynn, and she introduced them. "She says her name is Featherly. And that's... Deerla." There was a third fairy named Harelow. "The

pixies protect the Enchanted Forest. They're very magical."
She told Darling that the pixies wanted to help her.

Deerla picked a few leaves from the bush and rubbed
them on Darling's ankle.

"Deerla says that should heal you!" Ashlynn said.

Darling was better! She played a game of hop with the
pixies until Raven stepped into the sunlight. "Please help us,
Pixies. We need a place to hide from my mother, the Evil
Queen."

"Till we can figure out how to get her back into the mirror prison," Poppy added.

That reminded Darling, who asked, "Speaking of mirrors, has anyone seen my brother Daring lately?"

"I saw him at school lots of times. And at the Dragon
Center, and once in a dream but he was a goat..." Maddie
began.

Holly asked, "Why, Darling? Are you worried?"

"I don't like it. It's not like him to misplace his hand
mirror." Darling took out Daring's mirror but couldn't
see that Daring was screaming at her from behind the
glass.

The Evil Queen marched down the hallway toward the
dorms. Students leaped out of her way. Faybelle, however,
was on her heels, behaving like an overenthusiastic personal
assistant. "I need you to place dark dragons to guard every

possible escape! Nobody leaves!" The queen sent her away, saying, "Then come back to me.... Well? Flap off!"

"Yes, Your Horribleness!" Faybelle agreed.

Faybelle took her task seriously. She caught Jillian Beanstalk, the adventurous daughter of Jack, tossing beans out a window, but before Jillian and Humphrey Dumpty could escape down the magic beanstalk, Faybelle's dragon puffed a flame at them. They quickly climbed back up and in through the window.

The Evil Queen entered Apple's room without knocking. "Why the waterworks? Upset my Raven flew the coop? We'll get her back."

"Everything went wrong!" Apple wept. "This is not how I thought high school would be!"

The Evil Queen lifted Apple's face to look in her eyes. "Chin up, Applecheeks. Any idea where your roomie, my birdy, went?"

"I wish!" Apple said. "If I knew, I would tell her she was *right* about you and beg her to forgive me. You've ruined everything! I was a fool to believe you'd changed, or that you care about anybody's Happily Ever After but your own! Now the future of Ever After High is literally up in the air, and it's all my fault!"

The Evil Queen pulled a black apple from her pocket—a

single bright green worm wriggled around it like a tiny snake. "Poor, pathetic Apple White. I think our deal is done. Tell you what, since you helped me so very much, here's an apple from the teacher. One bite out of this, and you'll enter the next phase of your fairytale. Come on, Apple. Live the dream."

"Gross! I'm not touching that! It looks—poisoned!" Apple shook her head.

"Of course it's poisoned!" the queen said. "With the finest of sleeping potions, fit for the Fairest One of All. Oh, here—"

Electricity filled the Evil Queen's palm and morphed the apple into a fresh Red Delicious, shiny and crisp.

Apple looked at it fearfully. "But I can't choose my enchanted sleep . . . can I? It has to be Raven who gives me the poisoned apple!"

The Evil Queen shrugged. "If it leads to the happy ending you want, what does it matter how you get there? Think of this as my parting gift. Take it or leave it. But you are leaving my school."

"I'm not going anywhere," Apple protested, refusing the apple.

"Your usefulness has ended! Consider yourself hexpelled." With a blast of magic, the Evil Queen tossed Apple out the window. Apple fell a story, but then her ankle caught on Jillian's dangling beanstalk vine.

"*Whoaaaaa! Oof! Ugh! Whew!* I'm okay!"

Apple used them like climbing ropes and began her descent.

From the principal's office window, Faybelle watched Apple descend the stalk. "You hexpelled Apple right out the window? She could've been applesauce!"

"Nothing happens by accident in my domain. Don't you know that yet? I made the vines catch her," the queen explained. "Apple just needed a push to go find my daughter."

"Oh, very impressive, Your Rottenness. How can I help?" Faybelle asked.

"You follow her, you foolish fairy!" The queen pointed at the large, thick trees. "Report back to me. She will lead us to Raven's hideout, and then we will capture her."

"Aaaah. And what about Apple?" Faybelle turned to the queen.

"Here, take this...." The Evil Queen reached into her satchel and handed Faybelle the poisoned apple. She arched that one high brow. "End of story."

Apple dropped from the beanstalk and ran toward the stables, where she found her dragon tied to a post. She untied him and gave him a huge hug. After she put on her armor, she said, "Time to turn the page. I've got to find Raven, apologize, and get her to help me reimprison the Evil Queen. Talk about a twist! *Hi-yah!*"

Apple's dragon took off low through the stables, past the dark dragons in their pens and into the sky—flying away toward the Enchanted Forest. She swooped over Faybelle's head, not noticing her there.

Faybelle flew after Apple—flapping her fairy wings furiously. She was breathing hard. "I knew I should've taken a dragon."

CHAPTER 18

Apple searched the Enchanted Forest, uncertain where to find her friends. Luckily, the pixies found her. They motioned for Apple to follow them.

"Well, that seems like a sign...." Apple said.

As the pixies led Apple deeper into the woods, Faybelle began to follow, flitting from tree to tree. "Ugh, pixies," she muttered. "Wannabe fairies!"

Faybelle nearly got caught a few times, but managed to stay hidden. She watched as Apple disappeared behind a sparkling waterfall and entered the pixies' hidden woodland village, where Raven and her friends were hiding.

It was time to call the queen.

The pixies' village was amazing. There were doors carved into trees, balconies made of braided flowers and vines, hammock bunk beds, a stone fire pit, and in the center of it all—Raven.

Apple rushed forward. "I'm sorry. I was selfish."

"Go on," Raven said, curious.

"Your mom hasn't changed," Apple told her. "I had. And now I want to change again—for the better, for good. I've learned that a little White lie can lead to great evil. I know I can't turn back the pages, but I believe we can all have our Happily Ever After. But..." Apple looked at Raven hopefully. "But not until we stop your mom."

Apple showed Raven a picture on her MirrorPhone. There was the school, black, hovering above the earth, and covered with vines.

"And we will, my friend." Raven agreed to help.

⋘⋙

Faybelle called the Evil Queen on her MirrorPhone. "The Raven has landed. Repeat: The Raven has landed. Initiate Operation: Roasted Marshmallow."

"Okay," the Evil Queen said. "No need to speak in code. Plant the poisoned apple. I'll send in the dark dragons."

With an evil grin, Faybelle flitted into the pixies' village....

⋘⋙

When it was dark, Nevermore blew fire to create a roaring campfire. The girls sat around it, their Dragon Games armor flickering in the light. The pixies served bowls of nuts, berries, and a platter of fruit.

"Thank you, Featherly." Ashlynn told the others, "The pixies said if we plan to face the Evil Queen, we need to nourish ourselves."

⁓

Faybelle took the poisoned apple from her bag and slipped it onto the tray of fruit that Harelow was serving.

All the girls started eating—except Apple and Raven.

Apple said, "This is going to be fairy, fairy dangerous. The Evil Queen has turned half our friends and all the staff into creatures! The place is, like, a mile high off the ground and surrounded by dark dragons!"

"Then we need our strength. Here—eat up...." Raven tossed Apple the poisoned apple from the tray.

When Apple took a bite, it instantly turned black. She coughed and choked.

"Are you okay?" Poppy asked.

Holly gasped. "What kind of apple turns black?"

Raven knew immediately what had happened. "Where did that come from?" She leaped to her feet and whirled around, shouting into the dark while Apple fainted backward to the ground. Everyone rushed to help.

"Mother! I know you're out there!" Raven shouted into the forest.

⁓

Faybelle watched as Raven knelt beside Apple. "Apple, stay awake. Do you hear me?"

Apple coughed, her eyelids grew heavy. She grabbed her throat, gasping for air.

"Can you understand what she's saying?" Holly asked Ashlynn.

Ashlynn listened for a long moment. "She said how this fairytale ends is up to you now, Raven."

Darling checked Apple's pulse, then pulled Daring's mirror from her pocket and put it close to Apple's mouth.

"What the hex is that for?" Maddie asked. "Apple can't check her hair when she's—" She started crying.

"Quiet, please!" Darling said. "If there is fog on the mirror, it proves that she's breathing."

The forest went completely silent as Darling checked the mirror. It was fogged. And Apple began to snore.

"She's breathing, all right," Poppy said, relieved for the moment.

Suddenly, the sky was filled with dark dragons approaching, and at the front of the group, Faybelle was riding the largest one.

"Get Raven Queen!" Faybelle shrieked, pointing the way.

The pixies ran around in terror while the students leaped onto their dragons. Poppy's and Holly's sweet dragons were no match for the dark dragons. The girls got scratched and singed as the dark dragons pursued Raven.

Raven and Darling led the defense of the pixies' village. Raven drove back the dark dragons with a huge wall of purple smoke. She cast a spell.

> *"Dark dragons that attack by night,*
> *I cast you back till morning light!"*

The dark dragons retreated. Faybelle was dragged back to the school by a frightened dragon. "No! Heel! What are you, dragons or chickens?" She shouted back over her shoulder, "We're coming for you, Raveeeeeeeeennnn!"

When it was quiet again, the pixies handed Holly and Poppy leaves to help with the dragon burns. Ashlynn, Darling, and Raven looked down at Apple, who still snored.

"Do you think she'll snore for years and years and years and years?" Maddie asked.

Raven shrugged sadly.

A rustle in the forest got her attention. Four dwarves came out of the leaves, carrying a glass coffin on their shoulders. They lowered the box beside Apple and opened the lid. Raven shot purple magic from her fingertips, and Apple levitated into the box, where she could rest comfortably.

Apple's dragon sat at the foot of the box, to watch over her and keep her safe.

"Oh, I can't bear to see Apple like this!" Ashlynn moaned.

"She's not gone. She's just waiting for her Happily Ever After," Darling said.

"But it could be hundreds of years before she wakes up!" Holly worried.

"I wonder what she's dreaming about!" Maddie asked. "I bet enchanted sleep dreams are wonderlandiful!"

"Where is Daring when we need him?" Poppy said.

"He's the prince who has to save Apple with the awakening kiss!" Holly recounted the story.

"Where is Daring, indeed?" Maddie asked. "As they used to say back in Wonderland, 'Curiouser and curiouser...'"

Darling fiddled with the handle on the Booking Glass. Her hair swept over the glass.

Inside the mirror, Daring was going crazy and hadn't combed his hair in hours. Tilting his head, he heard the sounds of Darling fiddling with the handle.

"Hello?" he called. "Is someone there? Can you hear me? What's happening? All I see is blond hair! Darling? Apple?"

In the pixies' village, the friends each placed a flower on Apple's chest, creating a bouquet in her hands. Apple snored loudly at them. When Darling added her flower, she was still holding the mirror—which faced Apple.

Daring saw Apple in the glass box. He dropped to his knees. "Apple!"

Raven set her flower in the bouquet. "You apologized to me, but I never got a chance to apologize to you." She told Apple, "I brought all this evil to Ever After High. As soon as I realized I didn't want to play my part, I should have run far away. Somewhere nobody has heard of the Evil Queen...or Snow White. Or even fairytales at all."

Maddie said, "I don't think there is such a place! Unless maybe wherever monsters come from or something. But who ever heard of a Monster High?" She laughed at the thought.

"Raven, you didn't turn the school into a dark fortress of evil," Darling told her.

"We understand, Raven." Ashlynn came close. "We all know you don't want to follow your mom's story—and we support your choice."

"Ashlynn is right," Holly said. "No matter what."

Raven was lost in thought. They all watched in silence as she formed a plan.

"I should've given in to my mother from chapter one.

Maybe I could have led her to a land far, far away...." Raven climbed onto Nevermore. "Maybe it's not too late."

Darling was nervous. She fidgeted with the mirror handle. It twisted in her hand. "No! Don't do it, Raven," she said. "There has to be a better way! Giving in to your mother won't wake Apple. That's what you want, isn't it? To save our friend? Only the right kiss will set her free—Daring's."

The mirror beeped. Darling leaped back. "I think I heard you say 'Free Daring.'"

"Who's talking?" Darling looked around.

Maddie told her, "Your mirror."

"Free Daring?" Darling echoed. She looked into the mirror.

"Okay, got it!" Mirrie replied. "Your wish is Mirrie's command. *Free Daring!*"

The mirror let out a *zap*, and Daring popped out! He stood there, in front of his sister and her friends, with insane hair, sticking up at all angles.

"Daring, that's where you've been!" Darling threw herself at him.

He pushed her away. "Don't look at me! I was trapped without a hairbrush!"

"The mirror! That's the Booking Glass!" Raven put it all together. "That's it! The way to capture my mother!"

"Somebody should have told the Evil Queen shattering a mirror brings bad luck!" Darling said, filled with hope.

Raven and Darling gave each other high fives.

Brooke Page addressed the Female Narrator and the Male Narrator: "And so, Raven and her friends set out to battle the biggest drama queen ever after.... Will they be able to take back the school? Will Daring follow his destiny and wake Apple? So much pressure! At least they don't have to study for hexams, too! I, for one, can't wait to see what happens, next chapter."

CHAPTER 19

The Male Narrator said, "Things were looking awfully Grimm for the students of Ever After High."

The Female Narrator explained, "And the darkest chapter in Apple White's story was being written. A cursed apple from the Evil Queen had poisoned her into forever-after sleep."

Brooke Page said, "But you know what? It wasn't quite time for Raven and her BFFAs to close the book and put it back on the shelf. Because Daring Charming had just jumped through—the Booking Glass!"

Daring issued a warning. "Please—I understand it's been quite some time since you've seen this face and you must be going through withdrawal, but take caution! Too much handsome at once can be a shock to the system."

His sister snorted. "They're not looking at you for your face. They're just shocked you jumped out of that mirror!"

Raven picked up the Booking Glass.

"Still," Daring said, "I can't be responsible for any handsome-related injuries. Everyone, please be careful and start off slow with short glances. Sips, not gulps, people!"

Raven was examining the Booking Glass when the dragons they'd brought to the forest roared. Cedar, Rosabella Beauty, Dexter, Hunter Huntsman, Sparrow, Blondie, Melody, Justine Dancer, Farrah Goodfairy, Nina Thumbell, Jillian, and Briar Beauty all rushed into the clearing.

Ashlynn rushed over and hugged Hunter, whose destiny was to be the next Huntsman. "Hunter! How did you—"

"Jillian's beanstalk," he said, sharing a smile with Ashlynn, who considered him to be her knight in shining armor even though he wasn't a prince.

Jillian explained, "A few of us were able to sneak away from the school while Faybelle was out with the dragons."

Dexter saw Raven holding the mirror. "Wow," he exclaimed. "Daring let you borrow his mirror? That's a first."

Raven explained, "This is no ordinary mirror—it's the Booking Glass. We can use it to send my mother back to the mirror prison." She turned it in her hand. "How did we make this thing work before?"

Darling shrugged. "I don't know. It just started talking, and then Daring popped out."

Maddie took the mirror and started tapping random

jewel buttons on the mirror's handle. "Helloooo. Mirror lady? It would be tea-riffic if you could make the Evil Queen go away.... Start doing mirror stuff!"

Mirrie replied, "Beep. Beep. Passcode incorrect." The mirror shot a tiny little magic bolt of light that zapped Maddie.

"Ow!" Maddie tossed the mirror, but before it hit the ground, Raven caught it.

"We don't have a passcode!" Holly sighed. "Raven, can't you do something?"

"Yeah," Poppy said. "Unlock it with magic or something?"

Raven frowned. "In History of Evil Spells, Madam Baba Yaga taught that the Booking Glass is shielded by dark fairy magic. I have no idea how to counter that kind of magic."

"Dark fairy magic?" Briar whined. "Spelltacular—all we have to do is hext Faybelle and ask her for a little favor. That sounds easy."

Ashlynn said, "I'd give my left slipper to figure out how to make it work. We have to send that Evil Queen back to where she belongs for poisoning Apple."

Nina Thumbell, daughter of Thumbelina, looked around for the first time and saw the coffin. "Wait. Apple's been poisoned?"

Hunter, Cedar, Melody, and the others rushed to Apple's side.

"It's true. Forever-after sleep," Raven said softly.

Daring realized something important. "Wait—this is it, Charming. You have to wake your sleeping damsel with a kiss—and it's Happily Ever After from here on out!" He turned to the others and declared, "This is all happening so fast! How do I look? How's my hair? How are my teeth?"

He grabbed the Booking Glass to check his reflection. "Well, hello there..." His smile sparkled.

Darling snatched the Booking Glass from him and handed it to Raven. She grabbed Daring by the arm and dragged him to the glass coffin. "Come on, drama prince— let's go save Apple."

Everyone hurried to follow the Charmings. But not Raven. She stared at the Booking Glass. "There's got to be somebody who knows how to make this work. Besides Faybelle..."

Raven and her friends stood in a circle around Apple. Rays of light streamed through the trees into the clearing. There was so much hope in the air. Apple's dragon looked on from the side.

Daring slowly marched forward. He took a deep breath. Then he pulled out breath spray and gave himself a little spritz, and took another deep breath.

Daring went to Apple's side and took her hand. "Apple White. You are my damsel. And I am your Prince Charming. And now I will fulfill our destinies...." He leaned forward for the kiss. "And complete our stories—and we shall live Happily—Ever"—he kissed her—"After."

Nothing happened. He frowned.

Daring tried again. "Happily Ever After," he told Apple, then gave her a quick peck.

Nothing.

"Ever after."

Another quick peck.

Nothing.

He turned back to the group. Daring's face turned to panic.

"Daring? Is something wrong?" Raven asked.

He walked away from the coffin, devastated. "I'm not the prince of destiny. I'm...not her Prince Charming."

"Wait a splinter! What does this mean?" Cedar asked.

"It means Apple's forever sleep," Raven said, staring at Daring's back, "really is forever after."

Apple's dragon let out a sad sigh.

❧

Hunter built a podium out of a tree trunk. Raven stood behind it, facing her friends. "We're here today to honor and spellebrate Apple White." Raven was so choked up she could barely speak. "She was a Royal. She was my roommate. And she was my friend. She was kind—she was loving—and she deserved her Happily Ever After."

Maddie reached into her hat and pulled out a hanky—

actually a long strand of hankies tied together—then she wiped away a tear.

Raven continued. "I wish I were as powerful as my mother—that I had the kind of magic that could take me back to when all this started. If I could go back, I'd tell Apple that she has a choice. We all do. We all have the power to choose our stories. And if your choice is to follow your pre-determined destiny—you have to trust that it will happen in its own time. And you don't have to make a deal with evil." Suddenly Raven had an idea. "Make a deal with evil..." she repeated.

Raven looked down at the podium—the Booking Glass was lying there, faceup. She gently touched it. "I—I have to go," she said at last.

Darling ran after Raven.

"Raven! Raven, stop!" Darling hurried to catch up with Raven. "Where are you going?"

"To make sure the rest of my friends don't end up like Apple," Raven told her.

Darling said, "You're going to see your mother, aren't you? Raven, you can't!"

"It's the only way." She handed Darling the Booking Glass. "I know what I'm doing. Here. You're going to need this."

"The Booking Glass? But we don't know how to—"

"Trust me. Somebody is about to have a change of heart."

Raven closed her eyes for a moment. Then, without another word, she hurried away.

Confused, Darling watched Raven go.

Nevermore and Raven soared high above the Enchanted Forest. The two of them were headed back to Ever After High.

CHAPTER 20

"A ttention, subjects! Your attention please!" The Evil Queen's voice boomed through the forest clearing.

Justine Dancer, daughter of the twelfth dancing princess, took out her MirrorPhone. The Evil Queen's face was on the screen. "Oh my fairy godmother, the Evil Queen is on my MirrorPhone."

Farrah Goodfairy, daughter of a fairy godmother, looked at her MirrorPhone. "Mine too!"

In fact, the Evil Queen was MirrorCasting to everyone.

"Just thought you'd be hexcited to know that I am leaving Ever After High, and this kingdom forever after," she announced. She paused for effect, then said, "That's right, your cursed little lives have all been spared because—well, let's just say Mother's Day came early this year." She laughed, giddy with joy.

"My daughter, Raven Queen, has agreed to join me by

my side." Raven stood next to her mother in the frame. She was now dressed in an evil-looking black dress. "To become evil and take over other lands with me—on the condition that I leave this kingdom and never return."

The students, at the school and in the forest, all reacted with horror.

"Raven, no!"

"Raven's going to be evil?"

"Raven joined the Evil Queen?"

Everyone was speaking at once.

On the screen, the Evil Queen put her arm around her daughter. "I tell you, the girl drives a hard bargain. But then again, I think we all know where she gets that from."

Darling looked at her MirrorPhone. She glanced from the phone in one hand to the Booking Glass in the other. "What are you up to, Raven Queen?"

Raven stood with her mother in what used to be her school. She glanced over at Faybelle, who was sitting in the corner. The floating castle was nothing like its former self. The halls were dark, and menacing black dragons swooped the grounds on guard duty.

The queen looked at a map of all the fairytale lands.

"Let's see here…what land shall we take over first?" She cackled. "We could take another crack at Wonderland—that's an old favorite. Ooh, ooh, or we could conquer and rule over Gingerbread Land. That could be sweet. Or—or—hear me out now—the Land of the Giants!"

Raven was anxious. "Those all sound great, Mom. I'll go anywhere you want. As long as it's not here."

"Ah! I'm too excited to pick. My wicked little blackbird has flown home. Mother-daughter evil selfie!" The Evil Queen cast a spell and pulled Raven across the room and into her arms. She tugged her close with one arm, reaching out the other with a MirrorPhone and snapping a picture.

Faybelle rolled her eyes. "Oh my fairy godmother!"

"Is there a problem, Faybelle?" The queen turned.

Faybelle marched across the room with heavy steps. "I've spent all this time fluttering around, doing your evil bidding without so much as a 'Hey, thanks, Faybelle. Hex of a job.'"

The Evil Queen arched an eyebrow.

"And now little Miss…" Faybelle mocked Raven. "*I'm gonna choose my own destiny* comes waltzing in, and you actually believe she's going to be evil!"

The Evil Queen said to Raven, "Will you excuse us for one moment?" Snapping her fingers, a soundproof glass box appeared around her and Faybelle.

❧

Inside the box, the queen shouted, "That is my daughter you're talking about!"

"Whatever after. I'm telling you"—Faybelle glanced through the glass—"she is up to something. You don't honestly think she's evil now."

"Maybe not now, but she will learn. The important thing is that she's here. With me. Where she belongs." The queen began shouting as the argument grew more heated. "She's going to be just like me because I gave her no choice! All my plotting and planning has finally gotten me what I want! Don't you understand? I won!"

"All this was about Raven?" Faybelle looked outside the box at Raven. Then back to the Evil Queen. "But—what about me?"

"What about you?" The queen's voice was high and fierce.

Faybelle turned away. She was hurt. Sometimes it seemed like feeling left out was part of her destiny.

The Evil Queen snapped her fingers and the soundproof box disappeared.

Faybelle stared at Raven and the Evil Queen standing together. Her face flickered from hurt to angry, and, with a final realization that she had been used, Faybelle stormed out of the office.

From the corner of her eye, Raven saw the change in Faybelle.

"Hey, what the hex?" Daring exclaimed as Darling pulled him to his feet and dragged him along with her. "Can't you see I'm trying to wallow?"

Darling wasn't going to let him sit around all day. "All this pouting—not a good look on you. It's time to turn the page, brother."

"That's easy for you to say," Daring told her. "Don't you understand? I just lost my destiny. I'm not Apple's Prince Charming!"

Darling said, "And I'm not a damsel in distress! Some of us aren't going to follow our original destinies."

"Raven did," Daring said. "Nobody ever thought she would, but look what happened."

Darling shook her head. Her brother was so dense sometimes. "Raven did what she had to do to save her friends. She had a choice to make. And so do you."

Daring looked completely defeated. "I was so sure I was Apple's Prince Charming. If my kiss can't wake her, then I don't know what can."

At that moment, Apple shot up and opened her eyes. Then she immediately collapsed. Darling rushed over to her side. She tried to listen to her heartbeat.

Suddenly Darling had an idea. Clasping her hands together, she placed them on Apple's chest and began to press hard, in perfect medical form.

"Darling? What are you—" Briar started.

Darling explained, "The poisoned apple. It's still in her throat!"

"Come on. Come on!" Darling chanted as she worked. One final compression and the piece of apple was forced out of Apple's mouth—it vaporized instantly in a wisp of purple magic.

Darling bent down and put her cheek next to Apple's mouth. "Breathe, Apple!"

Apple started coughing, then...she sat up! Her dragon let out a blast of celebration ice! It sparkled white and cold.

"What happened? Did—did Daring wake me up?" Apple asked, confused.

Daring shook his head. "No," he said, and blushed awkwardly.

It was then that Apple looked around at all the welcoming faces and realized someone was missing. "Wait," she said. "Where's Raven?"

CHAPTER 21

Apple was pacing the forest clearing. "Un-hexceptable! The Evil Queen cannot be allowed to win like this. We have to do something."

Ashlynn said, "I'm sorry, Apple—but I think we're too late."

"You don't understand," Apple cried. "This is all my fault. I set the Evil Queen free." This was surprising news to her friends. "I thought keeping her secret was going to be good for Ever After High. Good for all of us." She went on, "But look at all the trouble it led to. And Raven joining sides with her mother? That's not the Happily Ever After she wanted."

Apple begged her friends, "Please. Help me fight back and save Raven. We have dragons! We have the Booking Glass. We just need the passcode."

"We've tried, Apple," Darling told her. "But we can't

guess the combination. Daring just got lucky when he got captured."

Daring was offended. "I wouldn't put it *that* way."

From the side of the clearing, the dragons began to roar as a shadow approached.

It was Faybelle riding a dark dragon. She descended and landed with a dramatic thud. Faybelle leaped to the ground. With a flick of her wrists, her dragon companion was dismissed and flew away. "Let me guess. Can't figure out how to use the Booking Glass?"

Everyone watched as she went to take the Booking Glass from Darling. Darling gripped the mirror for a beat, unsure if she should trust Faybelle. Finally, she let go, and Faybelle took the mirror. She twirled it in her hands and chanted, "Ready? Okay! *One, two, three, four—the Booking Glass is locked no more!*"

The magic mirror glowed.

"What shall I capture?" Faybelle looked around and saw Sparrow holding a sandwich. Faybelle aimed the mirror to reflect it in the glass, then pressed the jewel sequence.

"*Dootle-doot*," Mirrie said, turning on. "*Beep. Beep.* Capturing sandwich." Magic energy shot out of the mirror at the sandwich, grabbed it, and pulled it back into the mirror. A moment later, it was gone.

With a satisfied smile, Faybelle gave the mirror back to Darling.

Darling asked, "I don't understand. Why are you switching sides?"

"You're not going to be evil anymore?" Apple didn't trust her.

"*Psh*—oh, I'm still waaay evil...." Faybelle said with a laugh. "This dark fairy is just out for revenge. I worked my wings off for that ungrateful queen. Let's see how well her wicked plans go without Faybelle in her corner." No one moved. "Well, what are you waiting for, people? Do I have to do everything for you? Dragon up!"

As everybody scrambled to mount their dragons, Apple noticed Darling at the edge of the clearing, studying the Booking Glass. Apple went to her.

"Somebody is going to have a change of heart," Darling said softly. "That's what Raven told me before she left."

"What does that mean?" Apple asked.

Neither of them had a clue. But Briar Beauty understood. "It means that she knew Faybelle was going to get angry at the Evil Queen and switch sides."

Ashlynn smiled. "This was part of her plan all along. She's playing her mother."

"And she knows that we're coming with the Booking Glass." Darling hurried to her dragon.

At Ever After High, Raven stared out the window, searching the horizon. There was nothing to be seen. Not yet.

She turned to see her mother packing her spell ingredients, moving them from a big cabinet and into a small suitcase. In the corner of her eye, she saw that Raven was staring again out the window. "Why do you keep doing that?"

"Huh? Doing...what?" Raven asked.

"Looking out the window. What are you looking for?" The Evil Queen stepped over to scan the skies.

"I—nothing." Raven tore her eyes back to her mom. "I'm just...really hexcited about being evil and conquering the world...and stuff."

The Evil Queen looked suspiciously at Raven. "Prove it," she told her daughter. With a tip of her staff, a swirling black portal appeared on the floor.

"What do you mean?" Raven asked.

"You're on the path to become evil now, dear," the Evil Queen said. "Toss Snow White and those amphibious teachers into that void."

Raven was scared. A quick glance out the window told her no one was coming. With great uncertainty, she stepped to the terrarium. The creature teachers looked up at her, and Raven shook her head. She wouldn't hurt them.

Thinking fast, she tossed magic at the Evil Queen, but her mother was faster. The queen blasted Raven with her own spell, freezing her in place. Raven couldn't move.

"I know you're just doing all this to save your little friends out there," the queen hissed. "You may not be evil now, Raven Queen, but mark my words—I am much more powerful than you—and you will learn!"

A dragon screeched outside the castle.

The Evil Queen swung around, her cloak billowing. "What was that?" To take a closer look, the queen created bubble binoculars. It was the Ever After High students on dragonback, led by Apple White.

"Apple. Apple's awake!" Raven breathed with relief.

Through the bubbles, the queen could see that Apple was gripping the Booking Glass. It had been activated and was shimmering with magic. The queen also saw Faybelle sporting an evil grin on her dark dragon.

"Yes...and it seems somebody showed her how to use the Booking Glass." The queen was furious. She yelled at Raven, "You! You were behind this! You played on Faybelle's jealousies and tricked her into joining your friends." Raven winced in fear as her mother got very close and breathed, "That—makes—me—so proud of you!"

Raven blinked hard. "Huh?"

The queen clapped her hands. "You manipulative little chip off the old glass slipper! It takes a truly wicked mind to concoct a scheme like that. Oh! You have so much potential!" She gave her daughter's cheeks a little pinch. "It's too bad I have to go destroy your friends now," she said, and with a flick of her wrist, the whole wall of the headmaster's office tore away from the building, leaving a huge, gaping hole to the outside. A cold wind blew through the building.

The queen cackled, her evil voice echoing, "Spell you later." She leaped through the hole, landing on a dark dragon. Two other dark dragons moved in to flank her like fighter pilots.

Raven was still frozen by magic. Her eyes darted over to the creature teachers in the terrarium. She felt the need to explain. "Our relationship is...complicated."

CHAPTER 22

The students rode their dragons in formation: five light dragons, Legend, and the three dark dragons who were under Faybelle's control. The students had doubled up for the ride back to school.

Apple brought her dragon up next to Faybelle's and asked, "How close do I have to be for the Booking Glass to work?"

"Fairy close!" Faybelle called back.

"All right, everyone—hang on to your crowns!" Darling whipped her reins, and her dragon lurched forward with more speed. The other students did the same, and their dragons flapped their wings—everyone was prepared to take on the queen.

"Ready? *Fire!*" Darling commanded.

Some dragons let out blasts of fire. Others shot ice. The battle for the school had begun.

The Evil Queen held out her hand and captured the fire and ice blasts.

She laughed at the attacking force, saying, "It's so cute you think you can take on the greatest dragon rider in the history of Ever After High! Good luck with that!" Then, "*Fire!*"

Her dark dragons unleashed their power at the Ever After High dragons.

"Spread out!" Darling ordered her troops.

The students scattered as they pulled their dragons left, right, and into nosedives, narrowly missing the explosive blasts!

The Evil Queen's dragons picked up speed as they each turned off to pursue individual dragons in one-on-one fights.

Raven was watching the battle from the massive hole in the side of the school. She struggled to move, but she was completely frozen with magic. Blasts of fire and ice flickered amid the chaotic aerial skirmish.

She closed her eyes and concentrated. It was difficult, painful....Raven gritted her teeth—and suddenly a wisp of purple magic smoked from her fingers. Beads of sweat dripped from her brow as she fought harder, and then...her mother's freeze magic shattered!

Snake Snow White and the other creature teachers leaped, crawled, and slithered with joy.

Raven whistled for Nevermore. A moment later, she was off into the sky, joining her friends in battle.

※

It was chaos in the skies. Apple was trying to get close enough to the Evil Queen to use the Booking Glass. "Capture the Evil Queen!" Apple shouted against the wind.

"*Beep. Beep*," Mirrie said. "Capture Beagle Spleen. *Beep. Beep*. I don't know what that is."

The Evil Queen laughed maniacally.

The queen sent her dragon into a spiraling tailspin to try to outmaneuver Apple's dragon—but Apple mimicked the move and stuck close on her tail. As they spiraled down, explosions of fire and ice blasted around them.

"Come on! I thought we were BFFAs! Remember the good times, Apple?" The queen loved the chase.

Apple clicked the jewels on the mirror, and it refreshed with magic.

The Evil Queen slowed her dragon and made a U-turn. She flew directly toward Apple....

"Capture the *Evil Q*—" Apple started, but then shouted "*No!*" as the Evil Queen used a bolt of magic to snag the mirror right out of Apple's hand.

The queen reined her dragon to a stop and spun the mirror in her hand.

Mirrie beeped. "I'm sorry, target unclear."

Apple gritted her teeth.

The Evil Queen circled around Apple's dragon. "Now I'm going to let all your friends see what it's like to spend years in the mirror prison. Starting with you!" The mirror clicked. "Capture Appl—"

She didn't finish, because a bolt of lightning struck the Evil Queen's hand! With a scream, she dropped the mirror, and it fell fast.

The bolt was from Raven on Nevermore. Her fingers still glowed.

"Hitting a moving target on dragonback—somebody's been practicing!" The Evil Queen was impressed.

Apple took a nosedive and caught the falling Booking Glass moments before it hit the ground.

"It's over, Mom," Raven announced. "We're taking back the school."

The Evil Queen sneered.

Apple said, "I let you out of the mirror prison—and now I'm going to send you back." She held the mirror, pointing at the queen.

The queen raised an eyebrow. "You might want to think about what you're doing, Apple. You're throwing away your destiny."

"Don't listen to her, Apple," Raven warned.

The queen said, "Without me, you'll never get your Happily Ever After. Raven has made it abundantly clear that she doesn't intend to follow in my footsteps. You'll never

have an Evil Queen if I'm not around. No Evil Queen—no Happily Ever After."

With all that said, Apple still didn't lower the mirror.

"Face it," the queen told her. "You don't have a choice."

Apple looked at Raven, then back at the queen. "Yes, I do. We all have a choice. And I'll find my Happily Ever After some other way—without you." She spoke more clearly than ever before. *"Capture Evil Queen!"*

The mirror finally understood.

CHAPTER 23

Magic from the mirror reached out and grabbed the Evil Queen!

The queen got sucked halfway into the mirror—her legs were trapped, but from the waist up, she was still free. "I'm—not—going—back!" She shot constant magic at the Booking Glass.

The Evil Queen's magic radiated through the mirror and into Apple!

Raven panicked. "Apple!"

"She's—she's weakening the Booking Glass!" Apple shouted back.

As the Evil Queen kept shooting magic, she started to emerge from the mirror.

Raven leaped from Nevermore and onto Apple's dragon to help her. Raven's hands lit up when she started shooting her own magic at the Booking Glass to counter her mother's magic.

The Evil Queen was slowly pulled back into the mirror again. But she fought it. "I told you! I'm—more—powerful than you!" There was a huge burst of magic energy that sent Raven, Apple, and the mirror falling off the dragon. They went into a free fall!

Apple was still clutching the mirror as the Evil Queen tried to escape its magnetic pull. The girls plummeted closer and closer to the ground.

"Raven!" Apple warned. "The mirror isn't strong enough without you!"

Trying to ignore the fact that she was falling fast, Raven took a deep breath and let out an enormous blast of magic at the mirror. Her magic increased the strength of the mirror's pull.

"*Nooooo!*" The Evil Queen was overpowered, and a second later, she disappeared into the reflective glass.

Raven and Apple were just about to hit the ground...when Darling swooped down on dragonback and caught them both!

They rose victoriously into the air.

Below them, the Booking Glass smashed into the ground and shattered into a million pieces.

In the Ever After High headmaster's office, Snow White and the teachers changed back to their real forms.

At a table in the Castleteria, Professor Pied Piper and Mr. Badwolf also turned back into their former selves.

With the leader gone, the dark dragons stopped fighting and flew away. And Ever After High was returned to its normal state.

Raven and Apple finally relaxed on the back of Darling's dragon. Darling looked back at them and exclaimed, "That was spelltacular, you two!"

Apple and Raven hugged while all around them other students spun their dragons with celebratory tricks and loops.

Brooke Page said, "You can open your eyes now, Dad. Raven and Apple won."

The Male Narrator said, "Wha—huh? I wasn't closing my eyes." He ended his narration by saying, "The Evil Queen was sent back into the mirror prison. And Raven proved that she—and her friends—indeed had the ability to choose their Happily Ever Afters."

The Female Narrator said, "With the help of her friends, Apple was able to right the wrong of freeing the Evil Queen."

Snow White nodded at her daughter with apologetic eyes. Apple nodded back. They embraced.

Brooke Page asked, "And as for Raven and her mother? Let's just say their relationship is still…complicated…."

After the spellebration, Raven walked confidently into the school's tower attic.

The Evil Queen was back inside the mirror. "There's my little blackbird…."

"Mom."

"So…what's new?" the queen asked.

"How are you holding up in there?" Raven asked with a small smile.

"Oh, it's not so bad, I suppose. Somebody left a sandwich in here." She held up the sandwich Faybelle had sent to the mirror prison using the Booking Glass. The queen said, "I'm royally proud of you, Raven."

Raven nearly choked. "Seriously? After all that?"

The queen grinned wide. "Hex yes, I'm serious! You demonstrated that your powers are even stronger than before. And to orchestrate such a crafty scheme to take down the Evil Queen? *The* Evil Queen."

Raven didn't know how to respond. It was all a little strange….

"You're more like me than you realize. Like it or not—you can't escape your destiny."

Raven sighed. "We'll see. I have to go, Mom. I'm late for a match."

"I'll be watching." The queen gave her a royal wave.

The Ever After High teams were twisting and turning on their dragons, hurling balls through hoops, and blasting fire and ice. Riding Nevermore, Raven lowered next to Apple and her dragon.

Apple said, "Hey, what took you so long? We've got a match to win here!" Ever After High was going against Fairy Prep School.

Raven simply smiled.

They whipped their reins and took off into the Dragon Games Arena, gracefully gliding around each other.

Game on!